THE FIFTH PESTILENCE

and

THE TINKLING CYMBAL &
SOUNDING BRASS

CLASSICS OF RUSSIAN LITERATURE

THE FIFTH PESTILENCE

together with

THE HISTORY OF
THE TINKLING CYMBAL
AND SOUNDING BRASS

IVAN SEMYONOVITCH
STRATILATOV

By

ALEXEI REMIZOV

Translated from the Russian
with a preface
by
ALEC BROWN

HYPERION PRESS, INC.
Westport, Connecticut

Published in 1927 by Wishart and Co., London
Hyperion reprint edition 1977
Library of Congress Catalog Number 76-23895
ISBN 0-88355-511-5 (cloth ed.)
ISBN 0-88355-512-3 (paper ed.)
Printed in the United States of America

Library of Congress Cataloging in Publication Data

Remizov, Aleksei Mikhailovich, 1877-1957.
    The fifth pestilence, together with The history of the
tinkling cymbal and sounding brass, Ivan Semyonovitch
Stratilatov.

    (Classics of Russian literature) (The Hyperion library
of world literature)
    Translation of Piataia iazva and of Povest' o Ivane
Semenoviche Stratilatove.
    Reprint of the 1927 ed. published by Wishart, London.
    1. Remizov, Aleksei Mikhailovich, 1877-1957. Povest'
o Ivane Semenoviche Stratilatove. English. 1977.
I. Title: The fifth pestilence.
PZ3.R2849Fi9 [PG3470.R4]   891.7'3'44   76-23895
ISBN 0-88355-511-5
ISBN 0-88355-512-3 pbk.

PREFACE

Remizov (*Alexei Mikhailovitch*)

In 1906 (Remizov writes) Seraphima Pavlovna (his wife)—

'. . . had found teaching work in a High School, a *model* High School.

'As for me, I wrote. After *The Mere* and *The Clock*, *Round with the Sun*.

'One day I met Leonid Semyonov at the Nicholas Railway Station; he had then left the Social Revolutionaries, and become a Tolstoyan.

'"Well," he said, "and are you still playing about with your little beetles?" and gave me a pitying look.

'I saw what he meant, and at that particular moment most clearly. It was like telling a drunkard. . . .

'But what was to be done; I could not withdraw from writing. . . . For writing and praying are the same thing.

. . . . . .

'Just then there happened to be a census of dogs and motor cars in Petersburg. . . .'

And Remizov found work!

During the previous year he had been business manager of a literary monthly, *Voprossy Zhizni*, which had begun to publish his first novel, *The Mere*, serially. But at the end of 1905 the magazine had come to an end, and hard times began again:

PREFACE

> ' This was not the first time . . . that had
> been before we came to Petersburg . . . I
> wrote, and Seraphima Pavlovna went about
> giving lessons.   Shame comes on me to this
> day when I remember it.'

But during nearly twelve months of 1905, while
Remizov was business manager of *Voprossy Zhizni*,
the Remizovs had been rich : Alexei Mikhailovitch
had quarters provided, and £50 yearly salary !

*

In a notebook of 1905, under 25th October, during
the famous ' Days of the Liberties ' of the 1905
revolution :

> ' When I read what is being done . . . the
> Marquis de Sade comes into my mind :
>> ' We too have something to show :
>>> ' a stake was thrust into the lower
>>> bowels of a murdered girl.—(*Tomsk.*)
>>> ' a house full of demonstrators was set
>>> fire to ; those who found time climbed
>>> on to the roof, then the roof fell in.—
>>> (*Same place.*)

.   .   .   .   .

> ' And in Ivanovo-Voskressensk a work-
> man was boiled in a cauldron.'

*

From the same notebook, under 28th September :

' At Vyatcheslav Ivanov's there was spiritualism. O. Dymov was medium; while I took the villain's part—scratched like a cat, and tapped like an imp of Satan. It was very terrible.'

*

To one who has seen that fragile figure bent over his table in that little room in the Avenue Mozart, where Remizov lives, in Paris—who has faced those kind, playful eyes, and heard the quiet, slow speech coming from rich Great Russian lips that curve kindly and ironically—these three passages from a small book of his reminiscences will be illuminating of the man.

There will be felt the fire within that through years of poverty and illness and mockery (' has that Remizov of yours been long in the lunatic asylum ? ' Rozanov was once asked of him) drove this man to labour over both the material at hand (our miserably savage twentieth-century world around him) and the material of the past (fables, myths, apocrypha, monkish scribblings), and from this variegated stuff weave beautiful stories.

There will be felt the bitterness of a man understanding; the quiet words like knives, not in expostulating anger, but almost with resignation—*we too have something to show*—when he speaks of the beast let loose in times of liberty.

There will be felt the impish amusement at human

delusions—I took the villain's part, *scratched like a cat and tapped like an imp of Satan*—the mockery which is kind, as the quiet words twist unexpectedly, now serious—now whispering wild phantasy,—or of that magnificent body, the *grand federation of human apes*.

*

But this is for those who know Remizov; and, after all, the great question is whether those who do not know him will feel these things in him, and thus understand him.

Remizov must in the main be read slowly, in a quiet voice, not hastening, weighing the words in phrases, allowing the voice to cadence easily. He is not like Dostoyevsky, who may be read hastily, stormily, each successive overpowering idea borne along on the surface of a torrent.

Nor is he like Chekhov, relying mainly on an ungarnished ring of incident; for in Remizov, in whom Russian prose literature matures, the story has taken on the structure of mature, or classic, poetry, when every element is precalculated and mosaicked into a preconceived form.

Remizov's manner of telling a story derives more from Lyesskov—Lyesskov of the short stories, not of the diluted novels. (But this cannot enlighten much, as the short stories still await translation.)

PREFACE

The Content of Remizov's Books

If in his manner we may find a forerunner of Remizov in Lyesskov of *The Steel Flea*, in his content Remizov takes up the labours of none other than Dostoyevsky.

His main concern is with the burden of life ; man suffering beneath this burden ; and human warmth of heart—understanding, tolerance,—the healing balm.

The difference between the two writers is in this :

Dostoyevsky was concerned with demoniacal suffering (Raskolnikov, Myshkin, the Karamazov family), and a demoniacal or hysterical way out.

Remizov is concerned with the sufferings that are more terrible ; the petty sufferings caused by puny desires tangled in webs of mean things—sorrows never elevated to the relief of catastrophe ; the sufferings of desperation in which people are driven to seek forgetfulness of the wearying hours of life to which they nevertheless cling. Remizov is concerned with the misery of the great mass of mankind, whose happiness is gnawed by petty considerations, and for whom the slight oblivion of the cinema or the bottle is the paradise to which their daily activity is bent.

Whereas Dostoyevsky extended love to his fellow men in so far as they were demoniacal, Remizov extends it exactly because they are not demoniacal ;

and Bobrov, the *fifth pestilence*, cuckolded by his wife, soon deceived in his adolescent idealism by the mud of the life in a provincial townlet, perishes at the end, defeated, a secret drunkard ; and falls, as a last despairing vodka bout kills him, to dreaming of *Florry the Whore*,

> of taking *the anointing balm of vice* with those he despises for their vileness, in the club of Stoudenets ;

because he had stood against the human way of tolerance and understanding, become demoniacal, inhuman, living his solitary life, the incorruptible upholder of the unbending Law.

*

The *Social Club* of the provincial market town of Stoudenets, with its hardened tippling, its smutty stories, its indecent songs, its ' sniggering and monkey guffawing '—this centre of moderate, but persistent vice,

> ' At one o'clock every one goes home ; it doesn't do to go *too* far,'

the picture of which cannot fail to disgust the reader (and perhaps frighten too by its alarming familiarity)—is this then preferable, is this then to defeat clean-handed, upright Bobrov, idealist upholder of the Law ?

Fyodor Sologoub, in his novel *The Petty Devil*, described too the horrors of a provincial town—and let us remember that in its general qualities the provincial town is a summary of the meanness of our civilization. Sologoub, however, caricatures. His one comment would appear to be irony; 'This is what civilization gives us,' he would say, and, fearing contamination, turns disgusted aside and spits.

But Remizov's more realistic picture is not cloaked thus in irony; in place of Sologoub's gesture of disgust some readers may claim to detect even a smirk of approval in the more unpleasant passages. Is it then with resignation Remizov draws what seems at first a negative picture; petty vice triumphant?

It does not seem so. In *The Fifth Pestilence* he offers a choice. Here you have garbage—vile, debased men and women, savage, for here is the root of the savagery of which is spoken; but they are *human*. There you have an upright man of ideals, unbesmirched by vice—but *inhuman*. On the one hand the lowest of the low continuing their riot of life untouched; on the other, a man of hope, falling because he had learned to say in his heart '*people are at bottom coarse creatures*,' and held aloof.

*

Remizov has a great joke, a game, a game of holding aloof, played with all his friends. And behind this game, that goes on now for nearly twenty years, there is something of bitter seriousness.

A world-wide organization exists; renamed, since the Bolshevik Government introduced its strange coined words for public departments, the

OBEZVELVOLPAL, or, in full,

Obezyanya velikaya i volnaya palata,

which is known in English as the

G.F.H.A., or

Grand Federation of Human Apes.

Remizov is the Clerk of this organization. He issues Charters, signed by the tail of King Assyka I., appointing to the various degrees of the order. The Charters are made out in the form of ancient Russian *gramotas*, in ornate monkish writing, and each of them is a curious work of art.

The concrete qualification for appointment is divulged to no man, but I will make bold to hazard (and Alexei Mikhailovitch will forgive me) that it is to have shown that one labours with the Clerk for this human understanding.

The whole scheme started in 1908, from drawings made in fun by Remizov to amuse his little niece in Moscow, when he passed through in the Autumn on his way back to Petersburg from the province of Chernigov, where he used to spend the Summer; but yet in its continuance and development can be seen an expression of the feeling of despair Remizov has, viewing the savage world around.

As if he said: let at least a few of us escape; animals cannot be so low; let us be human monkeys;

let us unite in a refuge against this world around us
—and in this game find some relief from the tension
of our minds.

Of course, the meaning of the game is exaggerated
here, but it will not fail to throw light on the nature
of Remizov's humour and japing, which is always
calculated and symbolic.

In reminiscences of the late Russian writer,
V. V. Rozanov, he apostrophizes his dead friend,
tells him of the pain of leaving Russia, even from
Bolshevik Petersburg with its dying horror, and of
first realization of the walls of hostility by which
Europe is more thickly divided than ever, and he
cries :

> ' Ah ! after all, Vassily Vassilitch, only
> the federation of apes, the little federation
> of apes, has done away with all borders and
> banners and passes and visas—go where
> you will, live as you find fit ! And how
> limitless it is, this little federation, knowing
> no frontiers ; just as, alas ! how meaningless
> —this too without limit ! '

*

But lest again it should be thought that Remizov
sees naught but the beast in man, he who sees the
beast with such clear eyes, and gloats on the unlit
depths of old Ivan Stratilatov's mind, and on
the vice of Stoudenets, let one more quotation be
made.

In sketches written in Bolshevik Petersburg Remizov says :

> ' I have seen . . . the cement of kindliness by which the disjointed and impoverished world is held together . . . even amid *that* in man from which even the beasts turn aside.'

It is this human understanding, this *cement of kindliness*, that is the key to Remizov ; and raises the dirty old clerk Stratilatov to a lovable romantic idealist, and justifies the love with which the dark side of the town of Stoudenets is raked over, while incorruptible Bobrov is brought to a contemptible end.

Remizov the Artist

In Remizov Russian prose literature finds maturity.

One characteristic common to all the great writers preceding him—Gogol, Gontcharov, Dostoyevsky, Tolstoy, Chekhov—is that these are not artists before everything else. Their first consideration is the propagation of a sociological theory, or the solution of a sociological problem.

Remizov, on the other hand, is always in the first place *the artist*. Further, he is the mature artist, for he is not only primarily concerned with the composition of as perfect a work of art as possible, but moreover concerned with it in a detached manner, not allowing his emotions to interfere with the construction ; selecting, moulding, and then mosaicking his material consciously. It is easy, in fact, to imagine him working as legend has made James Joyce work, with various coloured crayons for the various passages, to aid the mind in composing the preconceived pattern.

But although the first consideration is thus the *craft*, this does not mean that treatment of human affairs, what some would call the spiritual side of the book, is merely incidental. Remizov is no follower of the *l'art pour l'art* doctrine, in which, I take it, the material employed is of no consequence whatever, for the second great characteristic of Remizov's art is that it shall be immediately concerned with human affairs ; that it shall, in other words, be utilitarian.

Remizov is a child of the Russian Symbolist movement, which grew to its full power in the first decade of this century. The theorist of the latter days of the movement, Vyatcheslav Ivanov, the most difficult, and perhaps profoundest, twentieth-century Russian poet, preached the essential need for literature to be utilitarian. In Vyatcheslav Ivanov's opinion *utilitarian* is to be understood somewhat as in the Middle Ages. That silent member of the Symbolist group, Professor E. Anitchkof, mediaevalist, continuing research into this matter, has clearly shown in a recent paper [1] on the aesthetics

---

[1] *Učenyja zapiski : Russkaja učebnaja kollegija v Pragě*, tom i. : vypusk ii. 'Qu'est-ce que l'art, d'après les grands Maîtres de la scolastique.'

of the Middle Ages that then literature was conceived of purely as a *spiritually utilitarian* occupation; that is, that aided the spiritual development of the individual, or helped him to approach the divine *principle*. This conception was widened by Vyatcheslav Ivanov, who taught that through and beyond the individual usefulness of literature there must be a more general, social usefulness; and that in this function of link between the *individual* and the *general* literature is myth-creating.

But if Remizov is said to be a child of the Symbolists, it must also be said that he has grown healthily free from his parental influences. While he retains, it appears to me, the Symbolist belief in the individually utilitarian nature of his art, he has clearly left the hazy religious strivings to which Symbolism led such writers as the poet Blok, and has turned towards a more real appreciation of the life around him.

He has approached nearer the spirit that animated Classic Poetry, that 'human nature—whether viewed in action or thought—must stand out in clear relief.' [1]

The Composition of his Works

From the preceding it should be easy to draw conclusions as to the composition of Remizov's work.

Surrounding human life is the principal material;

[1] *Roman Poetry*, by E. E. Sikes.

matter from fable and mediaeval writers provides relief, comparison, contrast.

The material of life is apprehended never from any sociological point of view, but from that of the individual towards other individuals.

From selected material of real life the story is built up primarily as a work of art, and in a mature, classic, conscious manner.

To this end persons and events, though circumstantially *true to life*, for which reason Remizov appears at times to be a *realist*, are made symbolic in relation to the work as a whole.

In this way that dark-minded, dirty old villain, the clerk Stratilatov, jostling through the low Sunday night crowd on the boulevard, becomes, in contrast with this crowd, symbol of the ideal romantic lover ; and, in *The Fifth Pestilence*, the strange affair of the ass's ears on the Police Captain's head, together with the incursion of worms proceeding widdershins and bearing a spiritual message, must be taken together with other extravagant things as symbolic events that contrast with the eternal slough of Stoudenets, its immovability, its *hearts and heads of oak quality*—and therefore as omens of impending misfortune.

On the Spelling of Russian Names

In spelling the Russian names in this book I have tried to work in the best English spirit, which is that of compromise based on convention and tradition, suspicious of any all-embracing rule.

I have for this purpose placed myself, to the best of my ability, in the place of an Englishman of moderate education, acquainted with the present-day rules and conventions that govern English spelling; and who, hearing the Russian names pronounced, makes a reasonable English approximation to the pronunciation—which he thereupon writes down.

The attempt that is being made to-day to reduce our spelling of Russian names to a wooden rule of transliteration, letter for letter from the Russian, is symptomatic of a disastrous tendency of these days to bring codified *order* and *rule* into our healthy, complex English life. In the extremely important field of education, for example, we hear of examinations being unified, schools and universities brought nearer a standard. It is forgotten that the pride and value of our education has been its diversity and flexibility.

Has it not hitherto been the characteristic of our nation that we do not *boil things down* to codes and measures, but allow variety and the accretion of convention, in which has been our strength? Are we now to fail and show the peculiar inelasticity of mind of old age, or the fallacious levelling, self-called logical mind of the new barbarians of Europe?

The error of the professors who would thrust a

system of *transliteration* upon us, and thus into English literature, is to identify their purpose with the general purpose. We must separate the use of Russian names and words in scientific works, be it philological, physical, literary, or any, when it is necessary to indicate by means of English letters and signs exactly what was printed in Russian letters and signs, from the use of these names and words in literary works in English, when they should be so written as, while giving an English approximation of their pronunciation, to conform to the conventions and aesthetic demands of our system of spelling.

The present chaotic manner of spelling Russian names should certainly be ended; for scientific purposes, by this system of rules for transliteration; for other purposes, by a slow growth of conventional spellings based on our own English spelling system. Let us not forget our English mistrust of revolutionary methods and reform by legislation alone.

A conventional system of spelling Russian names and words can only be formed in the course of years, and before a convention is formed variations of any word must be expected to exist; are, in fact, in our English manner necessary in order to arrive at a sound result; but all who use Russian names and words in their writing should give the spelling sound consideration, bearing in mind the English evolutionary manner of development on which stress is laid here.

The following considerations, by which I have been guided in my attempt to find suitable spellings, will show the lines on which this should be done.

The basis is of course our English system of spelling, but the following characteristics in it should be noted :

we prefer a ' y ' at the end of words, such as *Bogoyavlensky, Dostoyevsky, Stroisky* ;

we have a great liking for doubled consonants, which are rarely pronounced as two separate sounds, and generally serve to close a preceding syllable and shorten the vowel in it, as in *cabbage*, but which now have an aesthetic appeal as well, so that languages such as Serbian, which will not admit of any doubled consonant, even when pronounced, as, say, in *Rapallo*, appear vulgar ; for this reason we should write *Vassily*, ' *Voprossy Zhisni*,' *Zatchessov* ;

we express the Russian broad ' u ' sound by ' oo ' in our English words (*food*), but we have, for words of foreign origin and for a number of words with a false historic spelling, admitted the combination ' ou ' as well, thus *labour*, in which we pronounce shortened ' oo ' more than shortened ' ow,' and *gourd* ; for this reason Russian ' u ' should be rendered ' ou,' as *Stoudenets, Zavoulonsky* ;

we do not like the letter ' k ' for hard ' c,' and in many cases it would seem preferable to write English ' c,' as *copeck, Prascovia* ;

we do not write ' k ' at the end of words in English, but ' ck,' and for this reason I follow our traditional *copeck*, although our increased familiarity with Russian names during recent years makes it very largely a matter of taste whether a word should be left with a foreign air, as in the name of the poet, accepted as *Blok*, or anglicized, as in *copeck*, and time alone can decide here ;

although we avoid ' k ' we are accustomed, through guttural Eastern names, to ' kh,' when I take it we pronounce English hard ' c,' but imagine an Eastern grating or rasping as in *Kubla Khan*, *Omar Khayyam* ; at the same time there are words in which, although we hear Russian ' kh,' we shall prefer to pronounce ' h ' rather than ' c ' in English, and therefore in such cases I propose writing ' h ' ; we shall thus write *Chekhov* and say Checov, *Spasso-khodsky* and say Spassocodsky, but I have ventured the *Rev. Hariton* because the Rev. Khariton offended in a name that had such an English air ;

we write in English both ' tch ' and ' ch,' but ' ch ' we avoid in the middle or at the end of words, which should be remembered (' ch ' at the end of words we are inclined to take as a Gaelic guttural ' kh,' remembering *loch*) ; therefore — *Ivanovitch*, *Zatchessov* ;

we have the sound of palatalized ' z ' as in *azure* very rarely, and, I think, only two ways of indicating it, which are ' z ' and ' s ' before long ' u ' (*azure*, *pleasure*) ; the sound, however, is very common in Russian before nearly all vowels and frequently before consonants, and the only way to represent it in English spelling is by ' zh,' in analogy with our English ' sh,' and thus write *Zhiganovsky*, *Zhoukov* ;

our earlier rendering of the hard Russian ' v,' which terminates so many Russian names, by ' ff ' has, I take it, been now generally superseded by simpler ' v ' ;

we shall use our judgment as to whether Russian names derived from Greek names should, because of our familiarity with the *sound* of the Russian form, be written as we hear the Russian, or whether we should be influenced by the Greek original ; for this reason we shall usually retain *Fyodor*, for Theodore, ignoring the *theta* in both Greek and Russian spelling ; but the name we may meet in a Russian household servant, sounding *Fyodot*, which is unfamiliar, we shall more aptly render Theodotus ; moreover, where such a name has ecclesiastical significance (as ' *the icon of Theodore Stratilat* '), the un-Russian form would seem more suitable ; in general it will be better to render Russian *phi* of Greek origin by our customary ' ph ' ;

finally, in the case of personal and family names, we shall, I presume, depart, whenever necessary, from any spelling we might be more prepared to assume, if we learn that an historical spelling exists.

These considerations make no claim of exhaustiveness, and a satisfactory convention can only be reached in the course of time by the collaboration of all who are interested in the maintenance of an

English spirit in our spelling, which is a matter of traditional and aesthetic (therefore social) importance.

The Work of Translation

In making the English versions of these two stories I have tried to be guided by the only sound principle, that the English version must be written as Remizov himself would have written it had he, remaining Remizov, possessed an English tongue and written of Russian life for English people.

I wish to thank three friends who have greatly helped me with advice : Professor E. Anitchkof, Prince D. Svyatopolk-Mirsky, and my wife. I only fear lest the work is still so incomplete as to bring their names into bad repute.

I am also extremely grateful to the Publishers of the book for their most helpful understanding.

ALEC BROWN.

BELGRADE.

CONTENTS

The English version is dedicated

to

E. ANITCHKOF

THIS IS TO INTRODUCE ESPECIALLY,
BEFORE THE BOOK IS BEGUN,
CERTAIN CHARACTERS OF THE TOWN OF
STOUDENETS

FROM THE HIGHER ORDERS

OLD POPPÁ—or Daddy—PAUL, Vagabond to the Town, of noble birth, one time of the Corps of Pages ;

SQUIRE BYELOZEROV, Chairman of the Local Government Board, who is suspected of unsociability because of his strange treatment of Vassilisa the Fair ;

FROM THE LOWER ORDERS

OLD MAN SHAPAIEV, Leech by Lechery, who heals by fornication ; and

OLD MOTHER SPINNILEGS, surnamed Philipiev, who keeps the tea-rooms (*the Kolpaks*), and does charms ;

FROM AMONG THE CLERGY

THE REV. SPASOKHODSKY, known as *the Wreck* ;

THE REV. PESSOTCHENSKY, turned out of his living for his unbecoming conduct : given over to the carnal delight of roast sucking-pig ;

THE REV. LANDYSHEV, for two reasons, as will be seen, called *the Plaguey Parson* ; and

THE PROTOPOPE, or Rural Dean, the Rev. Vinogradov, famed for his Birthday (or Saint's Day), celebrations, who has some mysterious joke about the roast lamb with *egg-balls* ;

FROM AMONG THE MEMBERS OF THE LOCAL CLUB (WHO WILL OTHERWISE BE FOUND SET FORTH INTELLIGIBLY IN VARIOUS PLACES IN THE COURSE OF THE BOOK)

THE VETERINARY SURGEON, Peter, or Petrousha Grokhotov, a grand plier of the bottle, who is of great assistance in various emergencies ;

THE CAPTAIN OF POLICE (the C.P.), Alexander Ilitch Antonov, who, after breaking a temperance vow, is the victim of an allegorical misadventure ; with his wife,

MARIA SEVERYANOVNA, skilled in the extraction of bribes for her husband, on the proceeds of which she has acquired certain pleasure gardens ; and

PRASCOVIA IVANOVNA BOBROV (the wife of the Examining Magistrate)—*open at all hours* ; and, finally,

ALOOF FROM ALL

BOBROV, SERGEY ALEXEYEVITCH, the Examining Magistrate in the Court of Stoudenets,

Old-Gobbet-Bobrov,
He who upholds the Law,
Falls by the Law,
Falls for Russia,
Is that vile and abominated Incorruptible
THE FIFTH PESTILENCE.

4

I

THE WAY OF MEN

In Stoudenets there is room for every one—according to his pocket.

In Stoudenets Bobrov is no freshman.

Fully twenty years Bobrov has been examining magistrate. Now, twenty years, that is not one year—what can you not get used to in such a time —yet in spite of that you can scarcely find a man or woman in Stoudenets, why, even the lowest of the low, such as *Old Poppá Paul* (former Page, beggar to the place), about whom people would talk with such hostility. And people always talked about Bobrov the magistrate like that, as if the gall of him was fresh on their tongue.

Alexander Ilitch is the Stoudenets Captain of Police, and hard at that, but still, he is not so bad.

' The master 's all right, except he uses his claws ! ' Philip the coachman says about his master. And old Loukyanov the constable just as good-naturedly, and not without a sense of importance, stirs his bristles : ' I have borne through with it, for I was at the Shipka Pass.'

The police captain's fist would fall bang from behind—that 's the way—and the culprit without more ado tumble along nose first ; or, sticking out the bones of his middle finger, he would clutch you under the chin, a surer method even than Lagoutin's fist itself—and the Rural Police Commissioner Lagoutin is a hefty fellow, and if in hearty mood he can give you such a tarara-boomdeay you go flying through the wall.

All his years in the service Bobrov the Examining Magistrate has laid a finger on no one.

Why, even looking it—threatening a man—but even such trifles were unheard of; when cross-examining, the magistrate's hands always lay before him on the table, the fingers dry and long, as if frozen there.

And drinking, too; no one ever saw Bobrov drunk; and who does not drink in Stoudenets!

The Police Doctor Toroptsov, Ivan Nikanoritch, is still far from being old, but, fruit of merry days, his legs are like stone pedestals, never to flex again.

Petrousha Grokhotov, the *Bird of Paradise*, the Veterinary Surgeon, well, it is all the same to him whether it is three hundred or three roubles, the chief thing is to get going.

Yes, and his benefactor, Adolf Franz Gleicher the Pharmacist (Petrousha, in order to please, magnifies the German as an orb of learning)—the chemist drinks a drink of his own preparation made from poisonous herbs and bitter mixtures, such a strong concoction, such a stewpunch, that in all seriousness he reckons himself the first of wise men and chemists, an all-round-the-world Mendeleiev.

Alexander Ilitch, the Police Captain, is also not

a fool at the glass ; true enough, when they got *the Devil's Gardens* from Zherdev, he gave the Captainess Maria Severyanovna a sworn promise not to take anything alcoholic into his mouth under any conditions whatsoever, and, for the present, he has kept this oath valiantly since Holy-Rood Day.

While the Cemetery Parson Spasokhodsky, known as *the Wreck,* falling into the temptation of the imp of bibulosity, drank to such a point that one day his voice ceased, and three weeks was the parson silent, unable to utter any word or to make any disposition, and his speech returned suddenly when his wife, who had tried all means to bevoice the old man, decided on an extreme measure ; and taking a twenty-five rouble note, that is to say, half a *fiver,* from the chiffonier, the old lady lit a candle and there and then proceeded to burn the note before his eyes— and the parson found his voice.

But what is there in that ? They all like their drop ; at home, and visiting, and in the club a glass is the prime pleasure, and they drink till daylight doth appear.

So really it seemed he did not drink, no one ever saw Bobrov drunk at his work, always sober in his office—and no one ever heard from his lips any of those unsuitable expressions that need not be specified. Whereas in Stoudenets no one ever fumbled in his pocket for such a word, they knew how to hew out a word ; and in this way right and left with the most *unfortunate* articulations did they brawl to the offence of the memory of their parents, and indeed sometimes somebody would express himself so *incautiously* as to be hauled off before the bench.

The Town Judge Nalimov, Stepan Stepanitch, the *Fuklorist*, will put the chain of office round his neck and rattle such words at you, such *eloquence*, you really cannot resist a suffusion of blood to your cheeks.

While Parson Wreck, from the day he refound his voice, calls every spade a spade and is not in the least abashed by place or person or time, and though he has never been to war he can really manage it like a sergeant of the line.

And the Clergy School Teacher Shvedov, in order to amuse himself, redid the whole of Polivanov's Anthology, together with Petrousha Grokhotov, in his own fashion and exactly to the tune of Nalimov the Judge—*for adults*, that is to say—and lo and behold off went that anthology in this extremely improper form from house to house, and the poems were copied and learned with assiduity.

Wildboar Vasya the Telegraph-boy,—although he ate the lickings, in another respect (thanks to his *appurtenance of asinine quality*, as Satchkov the Stoudenets Tailor put it) a most remarkable person, —was simple of heart and to this day believes that the favourite song of the club,

'Say not yourself 'twas used your youth to ill . . .'

sung in chorus, in the moment moved to emotion,

by Stroisky the Tax-collector, Pratkin the Agriculturist, Nyemov, Secretary of the Local Government Board, and Petrousha Grokhotov, is really a
Nekrássov song, and not a Shvedov *transcription for
adults*.

No, whom else you like, but you won't drive the
Examining Magistrate to the *hellast tortures*—he is
not destined to sit in the lake of fire.

Nor do you hear of any excesses committed by
Bobrov.

Anybody else may be sober enough and all you
will, but nevertheless suddenly take it into his head
to do something or other so outrageous you would
not recognize your own relations.

Tyazholkin the Shopkeeper—ready-made clothes
—well, just an ordinary shopkeeper, but he had
great mirrors installed in his shop and, was it in his
joy, devil knows why, or by natural impropriety, he
undressed and, just as he was, all naked, took up
his position at the cash-desk on market-day in full
view of each and all.

Or Poppá Paul, the vagabond, why, that loafing
lout, he is ready to do anything for a glass of vodka,
with his shirt to his waist and all his details exposed,
you cannot hide from him, he is like the bathhouse
besom twigs.

' Madam, you must pay sixpence, or I will bring
you to shame ! ' he will torture some typist until he
gets what he wants.

As for respectable married women, he says :

' If you are not careful I 'll shout it about that you 're a bitcher ; hand over a shilling.'

And they hand it over, there is no helping it.

It would be ridiculous to suggest that there was anything of this sort against Bobrov ; there were no improprieties, no extravagances whatsoever to his name.

Oparin is the Mayor of Stoudenets, with his own Inn, and it is there that Barashov, the Church Warden, has his rooms, and has taken up the habit of never waking but to the drone of the bells, and you can pour cold water over him or scald and skin him with boiling water, he will not open his eyes, and only by the sound of the trump can you raise him from his couch. And the Sexton of the Deanery Church Pharaoh lets blood to return the sober state by picking at his nose and blood comes and it appears he returns to his senses.

Ivanov the merchant, too, the late Maxim Maximovitch, traded in putrefied fish, and he got his knife into his daughter Zinaida and ordered her not to dare eat his bread, nor, when he died, to visit his grave. And all this he put into his testament.

Or young Zatchessov—young Zatchessov's marriage was the talk for more than a year ! On the wedding day, after supper, Zatchessov went out into the yard to take a breath of air, it was already very hot, and he disappeared. The next morning the question broke on every one, where ? why ? and the young bride alone, knowing nothing, weeping.

' He went out,' she said, ' to take a breath of air, and disappeared.'

They rushed off to look for him, hither-thither, turned everything upside-down, he was nowhere. The father made no stint of money if only he could be found ; he offered a hundred roubles, that is, ten pounds, to whomever found his son. They were looking for him till three o'clock, and then they found him, down by the Bear, on the very bank of the river, asleep under a boat. Indeed he had wanted the air—indeed he found it !

There are no extravagances to Bobrov's name, and he is clean-handed.

Whereas to-day you will not find many so wonderful, people take as much as they can squeeze.

To consider even Semyon Mikheitch Rogatkin, Member of the Local Government Board, well, the Tax-collector Stroisky has no other name for Rogatkin but the appellation *scoundrel*, and thus does he extol him straight to his face, saying :

' Scoundrel, my respects ! '

While the Holy-Rood Parson, the Rev. Ambrosius, sold the communion-cloth to the Old Believers.

' What,' he said, ' do I want with such a holy object ! ' and he sold it.

And it was the talk afterwards that those Old Believers paid a pretty penny for that communion-cloth.

Whether it is that life has become a hard task, or that there are a lot of men out of work nowadays, out-of-works that never do anything but eat the labour of others, God alone can tell, only not to do such things to-day is written up against you almost as a crime.

No, nor is there place in the fiery river among defilers and outlaws for the Examining Magistrate.

Not only is Bobrov clean-handed, but he is no embroiler, no petticoat tangles to his name, nor were any other shady acquaintances observed, and if only he were not examining magistrate his place would be officiating in the Tikhvin Convent in place of the Rev. Hariton.

It is common knowledge that Prascovia Ivanovna, the Magistrate's wife, is not a fastidious lady—open at all hours. And it is no secret for any one that only the first daughter, Pasha, is by the Magistrate, while the others, though Bobrovs, are quite unbobrovian, Anyouta and Katya by the Assistant Government Attorney, Zina by the Forester, and the youngest, Sonia, by the Tax-collector.

The Tax-collector Stroisky, the court-payer of Stoudenets, *Don Juan*, enamoured of telling the count of his *exploits* in the club and in all their detail, did not omit Prascovia Ivanovna, and to her he consecrated not a few evenings.

The Rev. Nicholas Vinogradov, Rural Dean, chatting once in the dining-room in the circle of his friends and acquaintances, admitted that Bobrov's abstinence was an unusual occurrence, and Bobrov a *Phenomenon*! while the Secretary of the Police Administration, Petroòukhov, skilled in the castration of cats, joking, you know, of course, in totting off all the Stoudenets official families, entirely excluded Bobrov, quite seriously considering it a case where in his speciality there was nothing to be done.

But this Petroòukhov is as bad a case as Shvedov the teacher, cast into fornication, transforming everything after his own fashion, yet the Rev. Nicholas is not that sort, he is wise in his grey hairs and his definition is indeed of the wisdom of doves : Bobrov was a *Phenomenon*.

But of course ! You have only to think a moment how in the vision of after the grave that place is described where languish sinners, adulterers and fornicators, the Kingdom of Fornication, so vast is it the eye cannot take it in and there is none greater or wider, standing firmer or stronger.

Which means that God himself so appointed it, and so it must be, and is it then a light thing, man turning this sin to advantage and use ? Old Shapaiev, man righteous and holy, walks not in the way of his own will, but in the way of the Lord and of love, and this thing the old man did, and not by

13

any gabblings of words, not by whisperings does he heal, by charms said over holy oil, by grasses, by the bean, by the twelve keys, like old Mother Spinnilegs surnamed Philipiev,—old man Shapaiev heals by fornication.

Bobrov is exemplary, nothing remembered against him at school or at the university or in his work, he is as pure as a baby's kiss, as the Police Captain said, and even Nakhabin gapes at Bobrov's canary that can sing ' God Save the Tsar.'

That *plaguey* parson of the *one day* church (that is, built in twenty-four hours by public vow after the plague had passed), Member of the School Council, the Rev. Landyshev—there is a hole for every nail—opened a branch of the League of True Russian People in Stoudenets, and the first thing he started on was a census of the credentials, so to speak, of all the inhabitants. And Nyemov, Secretary of the Local Government Board, long considered to be under police supervision, found himself on the black list of dangerous rebels. The former statistician Smyelkov, who for some unknown reason collected birds' eggs, also found himself there. Koulepyatov, Oparin's clerk, was also written down for singing the Red Flag. And the three school teachers, too, Sarytchev, Gloushkov, and Plykhatchev, because they subscribed co-operatively to monthlies and read them to one another aloud. And that japing Parson Pessotchensky, deprived of a living, too,

because in the first week of the Lenten Fast he
bowed down to idolatry, forgetting the word of the
Lord :

> ' because this priest gave himself over to
> incontinence in liquor and merrymaking and
> dance, and the singing of immodest songs
> and to the carnal delight of roast sucking-
> pig.'

But Bobrov—Bobrov did not get on the list.

However much Parson Landyshev raked up and
dug up he could find nothing criminal ; it is true
Bobrov was a rare visitor at church, but natheless
on Redletter Days he was the first there. The
Postmaster Arkady Pavlovitch Yarlykov more than
once opened Bobrov's letters and journals, both
driven by the ancient and incorporated customs of
the Post Office and by Landyshev's request, but all
was legal and inoffensive :

> The publications of the Archæographical
> Commission, of the Russian Historical
> Library, of the Society of Lovers of Russian
> History and Antiquities, and various works
> of the Academy of Sciences—these were the
> chief items.

Moreover Bobrov was such a rare legal man ; you
jump right to Lykov, and it will be a wonder if you
find anything like it ; Bobrov does not only know
all the laws by heart, the code of the laws of state,
but all the appeal verdicts of the senate too.

Nicholas Vassilievitch Saltanovsky, Local Government Board Officer, also a *law-worm*, at meetings only knows what he has inquired about the articles of his friend Bogoyavlensky, District Member of the Court, as to whether there is not something a bit severer—and it really seems that if it all depended on him he would deprive his own self of the rights appertaining to his position. But this is all a hotpot of ignorance, a hotpot of ignorance and twaddle. Why, now, quite recently, he sentenced a peasant from Koupavo to four months in the galleys, now where is that done, four months' galleys, as good a tale as the Ouripino L.G.B. Officer Kroupkin, who fines every huntsman twenty-five roubles, or £2, 10s. 0d. per hare! Bogoyavlensky the District Councillor goes mockingly 'cheep, cheep, cheep,' to his friend grown so rusty in the law; which, although it may be done good-naturedly, is still not quite the thing.

Whereas no one ever said *scat* to Bobrov straight to the face, well, and there was no reason to say it, well, and it was impossible, you would bite your tongue off doing it, or you would choke. He would show you how to peck back, don't you fear, he is not the sort you can wind round your finger, and he is not the sort you can tread on easily—he is a prickly one and quick of tongue and not a whit timid.

And Bobrov's severity, Bobrov's legal dispassion

16

ateness are such that he would lead his own father to the gallows if the law demanded it, would not spare his own mother were there some criminal deed, is ready to die for his justice, give his body to the wheel ; strong he is and adamant in his word and will steer no double course—a moth would break all his teeth on him, as the deceased Mayor Taldykin used to say.

As for accuracy, he never confuses an article, stop fits stop, letter fits letter, and the most confused, over-confused thing you give him he will fit into the statutes. And his tenacity is indefatigable —he can seize on a hair and he will worm his way to the root and bring everything above water, a regular ferret. And his nose is that of a hound— he snuffles the air, then off to the hole, off to the bandits' nest ; and he will come, and hide or not as you please, whatever you do you 'll fall into Bobrov's hands, Bobrov will get hold of you.

Who will find wits to catch the thief ?

' Bobrov ! ' Bobrov could do things no one else could manage.

It seems you would have to look long to find such an examining magistrate ; there are not many such, and, indeed, a monument ought to be erected to him in the square in his lifetime ; some sort of Egyptian obelisk such as the Governor Oladyin erected to his own memory as a sign of his services and a lesson to after generations in Lykov ; or else elect him honorary citizen of the Borough of Stou-

denets like the timber merchant Nakhabin who
goes to Lykov and back every day in his own motorcar. But what is all this about, monuments and
honours, what ridiculous nonsense !

There are four fearful pestilences ; these are
Perdition and *the Pernicious* and *the Rot* and *the Ruin*,
and the fifth pestilence of Stoudenets is that scourge
and annihilator of the human race, Bobrov the
Examining Magistrate.

Every time when, in the club or in drawing-room,
conversation was exhausted and playing *hush-hush*
was not quite suitable, for in Stoudenets the silent
man is accounted a fool, every time such stupid
moments arrived it was the Examining Magistrate
Bobrov who came into people's minds, and a re-
laundering of the Bobrov dirty linen would begin.
And since Bobrov entered into no relations whatsoever with society except business relations, the
most extravagant material for the courts and the
market and the courts again was accumulated from
all the scrapings and rakings, the rumours and the
eavesdropped slanders, and the scandal-talk mainly
concerned the relations of Bobrov to his wife,
Prascovia Ivanovna.

' Cockroach,' or in English, *cuckold*, is what you
will most frequently hear when people begin to
talk about Bobrov. And with what a giggling, with
what a leering, with what roars of monkey laughter
did they not pronounce this *cuckold*, though there

was another title more phantastic still than cock-roach, and that was ' *Old Gobbet.*'

There dwelt in Stoudenets a certain Istsov, a scribe, a man with a booth on the market, who would put your papers through the government offices for you, and he filled in forms on the market, and he was the cosmographer too, and whenever there was an eclipse he smoked the glasses. In his heavy cloth coat and his wide-peaked cap, with his turned-up gristly nose and his goatee beard, Istsov used to wander up and down the market, waving his long red arms—the left had been broken.

' I am like a pelican,' Istsov would say, squinting down at his broken arm. It was this *Pelican* Istsov who had named the E.M. *Old Gobbet.*

Pelican—the very thing, a real pelican ; but why, now, *Old Gobbet* ?

Everything on him shone, faultlessly clean linen, in everything irreproachable neatness, his beard evenly trimmed, not very short and not very long. befittingly, an even voice with no suspicion of a croak, precise, pure Russian speech without any of the high-pitched Lykov broad ' o ' or any of your Moscovian spicinesses, pure as it should be, and one and the same smile that would flash out and freeze there, and a rapid, firm gait — an officer of His Majesty's Civil Service — and when he stood up and when he sat down and when he held out his hand there was a wonderful assurance in him, just

19

as if at his back stood the fortress of Peter and Paul.

More than once Nakhabin, in conversation with the Governor, well, not exactly complained, no, but *mentioned* the E.M. and not very flatteringly. Nakhabin based himself on all sorts of Stoudenets rumours, and hinted that the Magistrate was somehow unsuitable.

The Stoudenets Marshal of Nobility, Babakhin, spoke of Bobrov as an unpleasant fellow.

That pestilential parson the Rev. Landyshev wrote both to Petersburg and Moscow and all his denunciations hinted at some secret activity of Bobrov's that simply could not be found out

> and putrefactive of the soul and from pride
> and superbity of mind proceeding.

And the Government Attorney Inspection too was not satisfied with the E.M., but could make no observations ; there was neither what nor why.

But yet as if by secret pact all felt the presence of something unbearable, of something wrong—of a stone ; and so enormous that had there been any possibility he would have tackled it and cast aside this encumbrance, this stone. And that would have been just what every one desired. All the tellings and reports and intriguings and slanders and denunciations and all the talking and explanations boiled down to one thing, getting the E.M.

out of Stoudenets. For no man was agreed to live in brotherhood and peace with Bobrov.

And more than once they approached the authorities, but merely damaged their horns. Bobrov never had increases of salary, never any decorations, but they could not get him removed ; the county court was always on his side, valuing a good examining magistrate in him.

What was the matter, in whose way was Bobrov, and how ; whose life had he ruined, in whose road stood ? There he lives by himself, neither entering into squabbles nor mixing himself up in any scandals, neither causing quarrels nor making the peace, neither engaging in christenings nor in marryings, nor does he quarrel nor make friends. He does his work and does it honourably, with all severity, with never a moment's softening, favouring none, giving way to none, knowing no one above him nor desiring to know. He needs no one, he complains of nothing, he bewails nothing and to no one, he does his work honourably and lives there by himself.

Well, what is it all about, then ?

He is righteous, lacking only the aureole of glory about his head.

What is he then ?

A hater of God, a seller of Christ ? An enemy of the Lord, an enemy accursed, the fifth fearful pestilence, the scourge and annihilator of the human race ? And this *cockroach*, this *Old Gobbet*, this monkey guffawing, this sniggering, these male-volent looks ?

What is the matter ?

Without doubt this is what it is, this is the matter, this life self-contained, this secretiveness of his, his *separateness* ; exactly that he is no one's best man, no one's godfather, no one's friend, himself, alone, he, Bobrov.

And it was exactly this that drove an ordinary fellow, with, well, cards and God knows what other peccadilloes to his count, and using his claws and a bit more besides,—drove, that is, the Police Captain Alexander Ilitch to desperation.

Alexander Ilitch contained himself, contained himself, I say, and yet with all his good-naturedness reached the limit at last and summoned the vagabond *Poppá Paul* to him and for a sixpence the vagabond, to general satisfaction, *let daylight* into the E.M.'s windows.

At ten sharp Bobrov is in his cabinet and at ten in the evening he goes up to his room. The clerk has a luncheon break, but he himself stays in his cabinet and drinks tea at the table covered with fresh, clean American cloth.

Piles of papers and forms on the table. Bobrov puts on gold pince-nez and signs paper after paper.

Beside his table a hollow has been worn in the floor ; that is where accused persons stand, many of all sorts are brought in. As for him, he sits there upright, his arms on the table, his fingers long and dry as if frozen there, and in an even voice with a motionless and petrified face he examines them and stares straight into their eyes, whoever he may be talking to.

The Assistant Government Attorney in Lykov is always abashed by this even voice and direct glance, but the Lykov Assistant Government Attorney—every one knows what he is !

Bobrov's clerks do not stay long, they cannot stand Bobrov's taciturnity, and Parmyon Nikititch Kariev, the present correspondent, is already looking for another place without staying even a month.

Whereas Bobrov sits there for ever—has sat like that twenty years without fail—straight up, a straight man, all petrified, and his collars are as of stone, and his voice, each word falling as a stone.

Every wrongdoer knew that from Bobrov's cabinet there was only one path—to the prison ; one path, no second, nor would there be any third.

And as he crossed the E.M.'s threshold every accused person said farewell to liberty, of returning home there was no hope.

II

THE DESERT WHERE LIVES
NO MAN

Sᴇʀɢᴇʏ Aʟᴇxᴇʏᴇᴠɪᴛᴄʜ Bᴏʙʀᴏᴠ is a Lykovian. He was born in Lykov, went to school in Lykov, married in Lykov, began his career in Lykov.

His father was book-keeper to the Municipal Treasury, was scrupulously exact and through his exactness was executor to rich people and handled big sums of money and everybody respected him.

Yet the old man ended badly, got into some money muddle and passed his last days in no employ.

His father's misfortune would not have been given such notoriety, would not have called forth so much noise and malicious pleasure such as is awakened against the down and out in people who have not known misfortune, if his father had not enjoyed such unclouded fame.

But this was quite at the end of his father's days, and till then his father had been cloaked in honour and glory and the Bobrov house considered one of the best.

In the Bobrov house you could have heard a fly.

Everybody walked on tiptoe, father and son and servants ; they had to think of Maria Vassilievna, whom even a fly would disturb. For Maria Vassilievna alone everything was done. Maria Vassilievna through long, wearying, painful hours would sit in

24

silence, fixedly staring at one point, motionless on
the sofa ; and thus Bobrov recalls his mother, that
his first recollection of his first bitter sorrow, preserved through all his life from his distant earliest
days, from the days when he had first learned to
pray for Papa and Mama and could not decide
alone whether he could and whether he should
pray for the shopkeeper Zholtkov who kept such
wonderful spicy Lykov gingerbread ; when he
used to take a pole between his legs and off he
would go about the garden, ride a cock-horse they
used to say ; when he used to build stoves on the
floor from cubes and once nearly set fire to the
house.

He remembers, too, the nights.

He would be awakened in the night by a sort of
piercing sob and open his eyes with throbbing
heart, and see his mother sitting on the bed and
beside her sitting on a chair or standing over the
bed his father saying something all the time, the
same thing over and over again it seemed, the very
same words, faster and slower and then, like a clock
ticking, evenly. And so on till dawn when his
mother would fall asleep and his father, wrapping
three blankets round her and tucking her in so as
not to leave even a bug-opening, would cross her
many times, a long time, listen long to her breathing
and, all bent, tiptoe into the next room and there
lie down, without undressing, just taking off his
boots, on the sofa, and in a sort of guilty way, on

the very edge, and it must have been cruelly cold, because even dressed he buried his head in the grey rug and tossed and turned about, legs drawn up, until he settled down in a ball. And such nights came again and again.

They did not come often, but in all their fearfulness it seemed they were often, and it was impossible to get used to them.

Little Bobrov never showed on such nights that he was not asleep, that he was not asleep and saw everything. He used to bite his lips to the point of blood not to cry, and he felt very sorry. And he was more sorry for his mother.

The following day, when, after the terrible night, his mother sat silent on the sofa fixedly staring at one point, he would keep moving about round her wheedling like a little dog, and looking into her eyes. And she would look at him and see nothing. And he would go quietly away into a corner and take out his bricks and build a stove.

Oh, if only in such moments he could have caressed her, put his little arms round her neck and squeezed her ever so tight!

Or had some one greatly offended her? Or no, not offended, but let her into the world like that; and there before her only unbearable night? Something stirred dully within his child mind and he was sorry, but there was no way out for his sorrow.

He would quietly take his bricks and build a

stove until his mother noticed him.   Then everything
was gay enough and the rest forgotten.

'You are an unfeeling man!' his mother once
said in the night to his father.   This he heard one
night, one terrible night; and from that time he
was sorry for his father just as he had been sorry
for his mother, and he began to follow his father
about with his eyes.   When everything at home
was well—and Maria Vassilievna was not sitting
silent on the sofa, but doing something, some
needlework, or was reading, his father would
usually tell funny stories and mimic everybody, and
Maria Vassilievna herself would laugh.   But after
those nights his father would be subdued and there
would be no talking in the house.

One day at dusk the boy went quietly into his
father's room; his father was not sitting at his
papers as usual, but standing in front of the icon;
there was a large icon of the Mother of God above
the table in his room, a funny one darkened all
over, with written on it in gold

My Soul doth Magnify the Lord;

his father was
standing in front of the icon and in such a queer
way, his head crushed down into his shoulders as
if he was trying to lift some unliftable weight,
and when he turned round, tears trembled on his
eyes.

'For Mama!' his father said guiltily, 'for Mama

to be happier, I am all right, I can put up with any illnesses, but for Mama.'

' You are an unfeeling man ! ' his mother's words would not leave his head, and whenever he remembered them he saw his father in front of the icon, praying for his Mama, and at the same time his mother weeping helplessly in the night. ' You are an unfeeling man ! ' his mother's words came again.

His mother had something terrible on her mind, and his father was guilty of something, but what her burden was or what his guilt he could not make out, and as he put his bricks and stove together he thought and thought while his heart ached from pity. And one day he put a shaving in the stove and found some matches and set fire to it. . . .

When he grew up and began to look after his mother with his father he understood that his father was the most ordinary person, such as there were as many as you like in Lykov, and did not gather stars from the sky and had all sorts of petty sins to his count, while his mother—there was not one like her in Lykov and not his father, but an angel of the Lord would be a fit companion and protector for her.

Maria Vassilievna complained of no disease and was no withered skeleton redolent of laudanum ; she was in full health and her voice was strong and ringing, metallic. Looking at her for the first time as

28

people usually look at each other when they meet
for the first time, with vision pre-prepared, made
shallow and unseeing, with shallow eyes, you might
well think, and people did think so, that life for her
was, well, all strawberries and cream.

But by fate she had been given *eyes*—you know
the sort I mean—and she saw clearly. And everything she saw entered her soul. And she suffered
because she saw everything. And still more she
suffered since, such as she was, she was alone, and
it is not easy to be alone in the world.

And further she suffered because people, without
whom life cannot be lived, approached her in their
own way, with their shallow common measure, and
contact with people did not soothe, but merely
wounded her. She tried to find something to do
to fill her days, and when she found it she soon
threw it over, because the people with whom willy-
nilly she had to meet had nothing in common with
her except the work, and were perfect strangers,
and it was no work, but an agony in that way with
strangers, and she failed to find a suitable occupation. For her work was the contrary of earthly.

It was only when weary from suffering that she
threw herself into various work, and because of her
state of suffering she believed that in this work
would be her repose.

She needed something to do ; and she knew this ;
but only did not know what she was to do, and she
suffered still more.

Many times she thought of going away from
Lykov somewhere to the world's end into some
desert where there is no man ; and preparations
would begin in the house. His father would begin
collecting what he thought she needed on her
journey. But suddenly the minute of departure
would, unsuspected, unattended, arrive, and Maria
Vassilievna stayed at home. And again there
would be terrible nights.

There was always a starting-point ; somebody
met, some visitor. In time there were no friends
came to the Bobrov house, his father had broken
off with them, one by one.

Or it would be some conversation, some word you
would think of no importance, but that fell heavy
on her tortured soul ; only through long years
could all the things it was even indirectly impossible
to touch on when his mother was present be realized
and committed to memory. And what innumer-
able other things too would excite awful fits of gloom
and terrible nights.

If you are wounded, even the care-free wind can
irritate your wound.

How rare a happy day was in the Bobrov household !

If everything, you would think, to the last trifle,
had been thought of and all the household orders
given out and her room put in order and everywhere
that spick-and-spanness that Maria Vassilievna
loved had been produced, all the things on her table

disposed as she chose and a full supply of water for washing prepared—cleanliness of person in Maria Vassilievna was carried to the point of disease—and everything was as she wanted, and you had only to stretch out your hand and it was there,—misfortune would come in from the other side.

The day would begin with it; either Maria Vassilievna had had a bad dream, or something she wanted had got lost just as she was about to lay hands on it,—a comb or a garter; and all would collapse.

And Maria Vassilievna did not have bad dreams rarely, and was simply losing things all the time.

The things were not lost at all, nobody had touched them, nobody had put them away without her: there they lay under her very nose, staring her in the face. But it was not them she saw; her eyes stared and she saw not. And all would collapse.

And every time each outburst seemed to her the final one that would be her end—her death; and each time she had but one prayer—death; and the household lived in fear of that death. Fixedly staring at one point Maria Vassilievna would sit silent and motionless on the sofa, and thus passed the hours, the long, wearying, terrible day. And his father at dusk would creep up to the icon in his room and stand in such a funny way with his head crushed down deep into his shoulders as if lifting an unliftable weight.

And then she would feel better; and all in tears

would beg forgiveness for making every one suffer, having made every one miserable. And he would want to carry his mother away thither, to the world's end, into that desert where there is no man.

And he felt a tremendous power in himself, a power which would make it possible for him to do that; in his own way. 'Mamotchka, forgive us, we are all guilty before you'; while his father would trot nervily about, kissing her hands, muttering incoherent things, tears trembling on his eyes, just as when he was praying at the icon.

In this way passed a troubled childhood, a childhood on guard, with one central thought, how to avoid upsetting his mother.

Though there were days when his mother seemed gay and his father, overjoyed, played the fool, the thought was never absent that this tranquil hour could in one moment by some unexpected ring of the bell or by some bitter memory such as might ever without warning flood up in his mother's mind be brought to a blank end.

And, without showing any one this thought of his, he kept always on guard, learned not to forget himself, grew accustomed to calculate every single step in order not, involuntarily, to set his mother to exasperation.

The gulf between people opens up, not when they exasperate one another on purpose, but when, unbeknown, involuntarily, without the least desire, they unwittingly wound one the other. Then it is finally clear that in the very fundament of things there is no bond between soul and soul, they are absolute strangers.

Bobrov was good at school, but did not stand conspicuous in any respect. He seemed to have everything, every gift, could do everything well, was fit for anything, gifted in everything. But as for any one thing in particular, any particular aim or any favourite occupation—any especial talent— there was none.

When he had passed through the secondary school he went to Petersburg to the university ; and in Petersburg, too, everything went smoothly, both his studies and his ordinary life.

His father used to send him money—not so very much, it is true, so as to have no need to watch his purse,—but he grew accustomed to calculate every- thing, reckon things out, and was never in need.

When he was in his last year the misfortune happened to his father ; and he did not see the old people again. Alone in misfortune thus together they left this life ; his father bent double, down and out, his mother with fixed eyes, eyes that saw everything, she all in suffering. The old man fussed about no more, stood at his icon in prayer no more. No more did she crave death, now at rest.

First his mother, and then, after her, quite un- noticed, his father, gone to his last sleep.

33

' How shall I leave motherkins alone ? She will have no one to be angry with.' Bobrov remembered his father's words. It was when once, in joke, he had proposed a joint visit to Petersburg to see the Emperor—his father had one sacred dream and on it slept and waked, to see the Emperor and without fail to talk to him, and about what he would talk he did not know himself, but in all probability about motherkins,—something like that.

Bobrov buried his old people and sold the little house and drew a thousand roubles from the savings bank (the old man had put this thousand away bit by bit, in the little book, for his son), and passed the civil service examination, and went abroad.

Bobrov stayed abroad one year, in Paris.

Life flowed as evenly there too as in Petersburg, he managed to experience everything, he wanted to find everything out, see everything, absorb everything. And he returned to Russia, not to Petersburg, nor to Moscow, but to his native town Lykov as an articled clerk in the Lykov court.

Through his father Bobrov was received not very friendlily, even unfriendlily and suspiciously, in Lykov, but his reliability and matter-of-factness in his work were soon remarked and three years later he was appointed Examining Magistrate in Stoudenets.

Bobrov married and went to Stoudenets.

He went to Stoudenets with the best intentions;

his year abroad in Paris had left an ineffaceable stamp on him. His work in Stoudenets therefore appeared to him as a great social task for the welfare, not of Stoudenets alone, but of all Russia.

The first thing he did was to try to get into touch with the local society, but his contact with it left a most bitter feeling. And, cautious, calculating, not once, not twice only, he put himself to examination.

'Perhaps he was mistaken? And if they all seem so coarse, well, in the *depth* of their souls, why, each of them must feel himself as he really is, feel it, know it, and suffer?'

But this prescribed question was smothered in him by another: 'Yet has everybody this depth, this praised depth of soul, the power of feeling?'

No, he was not mistaken.

'People are at bottom coarse beings'—this idea there and then was engraved in him. And never did he recall his mother, Maria Vassilievna, at such closeness as in the first days of work and responsibility.

Only to his mother the things sublime and pre-eternal were given and close—to him the lower world. He took her exquisite soul and her eyes with their vision as a measure for his judgment on people and pronounced his harsh sentence: 'People are at bottom coarse beings,' and soon he added ' and stupid,' as he added later ' and savage.'

So Bobrov began his active life, developing all

the qualities of an examining magistrate within himself, which are severity and disinterestedness and exactness and untiring tenacity and the scent of a hound ; and all this, all his labour, he laid at the feet of the *Law*. Whether the Law was good or bad he saw in it the only firm bridle with which to restrain human coarseness ; and in the Law, the Law alone, did he see the salvation of Russia ; for without the Law, it appeared to him, there could be no Russia.

Thus did Bobrov's active life begin.

To what ends it would have arrived in other, favourable circumstances, God alone knows. He felt an immense power within himself ; and this power did not leave him, but as he worked, grew, and it seemed he could have done the impossible ; just as when in his pity he had wanted to help his mother and carry her away to the world's end, to the desert where there is no man.

*

It was in his family life that Bobrov did not succeed. His life with Prascovia Ivanovna, happily begun, soon found an unhappy conclusion. Not thus he wanted it, nor so should it have been, but so fate decreed.

If his mother, Maria Vassilievna, was but *living spirit* (and this was to be seen in everything, in her smile, in her eyes and particularly in her lips, while her body contained just so much living warmth as

was needed for the life in which that spirit burned)
—Prascovia Ivanovna was an earthly being, burning
after her own fashion ; her eager, straining lips, it
would seem, ready at any moment to burst.

Memorable to Bobrov was the day of their first
meeting ; when they said good-bye her palm flamed
at the touch and as it were with burned flesh he
went home that day ; and from that moment only
of her were his thoughts, only of her.   And whenever
they met and he talked with her, her most empty
words, suddenly replete with meaning, were signs
for him of that being of her that had burned his
flesh at the first meeting.

And just as in his mother her inner self, the
living spirit, burning in her, enslaved willy-nilly for
all life, so in his wife her inner self, her *earthly being*,
fieriness, soulless blood alone, enslaved for ever ;
and this mystery is verily great.

Prascovia Ivanovna, thus gifted by fate, was
immeasurably desirable to the extent that, herself
desiring and acting, she remained her *self*, in the
root of herself—a good and beautiful animal ; and
she became unbearable, mesquin and petty, snarling
and envious, bloodthirsty and cruel, as soon as the
human being no longer nameless, the human being
complete with birth-certificate, the human being
with its definite place in society, came to the surface
in her.

This humanness it was that put Prascovia Ivanovna
on a level with the local society and made her

everywhere at home, a buttress in all the Stoudenets intriguing.

Prascovia Ivanovna was one of the first of the
ladies of the club.

She was a good housekeeper and she could shout
down any one of the market-women and make a
good bargain, and you know the market is a thief;
and it was as hard to cheat her as it is old
Mother Spinnilegs surnamed Philipiev, who, by doing
charms with beans and keys, has on those beans
and rusty keys set up a tea-shop—*The Kolpaks.*

If it had not been for Bobrov's peculiar character
Prascovia Ivanovna would not only not have turned
up her nose at *bribal gifts* brought, but would
without question have developed a real skinning
system, would have instituted the *way-out-of-it*, a
sort of tax on the Examining Magistrate's work,
and would have left the Police Captain's wife,
Maria Severyanovna, far behind; and as for Maria
Severyanovna, everything she has got has her name
embroidered on it in flowers and garlands, and she
has raked Zherdev's ' *Devil's Gardens* ' too into her
possession.

In the first year of Bobrov's marriage a daughter
was born. The home was rounded off; and the
E.M. and his wife might have lived happily on, but
the following year Bobrov's happy home disappeared.
Alone the name remained.

On the first day of Easter the maid, angry with her mistress—dissatisfied with her Easter present—stuck Prascovia Ivanovna's letters in Bobrov's pocket ; letters from the Assistant Government Attorney Oudavkin.

There 's an Easter present for you !

And perhaps it would have been better for Bobrov simply, undisturbedly, and obediently, simply, not reading them, to have handed those letters to his wife.

This Bobrov could not do.

That flame which had scorched him, vanquished him for ever, flame of the infernal regions—thunder and lightning—the great high seas—destruction—blood—with that same force had eaten its way like a knife deep into his heart ; and his pain summoned forth a curiosity of despair. With what despairing enjoyment he read through and through the lines that clearly depicted the relations of the Assistant Government Attorney to his wife !

He finished, he folded the letters as they were before, and he called forth his whole peculiar character, his stubbornness ; and, with no manifestation of his feelings, Bobrov handed the letters to his wife as if some trifles, as if a packet of hairpins, without any word.

From that day his life ran solitary and lonely ; former days, then, be forgotten !

In the household nothing changed.

Visitors came as before, more than before. More frequently did Prascovia Ivanovna have evening parties, more frequently did the Assistant Government Attorney Oudavkin drive out from Lykov; and everything was very gay.

Bobrov was seen only at teatime, and then again disappeared into his room.

A second daughter was born.

And when he was told that a daughter had been born to him he took the news with extraordinary calm.

He went in to his wife and, as restrained as ever, all of stone, went up to her. Then, sudden, hoarse of voice as his mother in former days during the terrible nights, in a cutting, dry croak that sent ice down the spine, he struck his wife with his walking-stick.

' A bitch can't help bitching ! '

He struck her with his walking-stick, and turned round and went out.

*

Now Bobrov was rarely seen by visitors, rarely did he appear at teatime—his tea was taken to his room. His converse with his wife was simple and brief, about money, about expenses, like a man talking to his secretary about his business. Before a year was out Prascovia Ivanovna was pregnant again. And then something happened that drove Bobrov finally into his unflinching life of silence.

Bobrov was awakened in the night : ' Madame is ill.'

Something, it meant, must really be wrong if she had called him ; since the birth of that second daughter when he had struck her with his stick he had not gone again to her bedroom. So thus for the first time he went to her at night, to her bedroom.

She was sitting on the crushed-up bed and did not raise her head, and was sobbing quietly, and there was something in those tears quiet and bitter that clutched at the heart.

He tried to talk to her, began to question her as a doctor questions ; what was the matter with her, what had happened, what did she complain of ?

She uttered no sound in reply ; one would have said she could not hear him.

They were alone in the room and there was no one else there but they.

He stood hopelessly before her ; he felt how his heart was crumbling, how faint his heart was growing. He was ready to help her, he would help her, he would do anything for her. And how had his hand been ever raised to strike her ? She alone for him, she all for him.

He stood hopelessly before her ; he felt how his heart was crumbling, how his heart was growing faint ; while she sobbed quietly, a frozen, fallen tree.

Then suddenly she got up from the bed, stood firmly, strongly up, bent clumsily forward, then lower, lower still, to the earth, to the very earth, to his feet. ' I know,' she said ; ' I know, I know every-thing ! ' she said in a stranger voice.

And she looked as if she saw everything, yet nothing saw, with her eyes burning, blind.

From this night Bobrov took to drinking.

He would usually sit at a book after his work and read till after midnight ; and then a moment would come, whether it was from the silence of night or the midnight bitterness, or the air, as Bobrov used to wonder to himself, though soon it was from custom, when he would close his book and drink. Then, senseless, he would lie there. In the morning, stupid still from vodka, he would souse himself with cold water and, faultlessly dressed, go down to his examining office, and begin his work.

And what assurance there was in every move-ment, in every word.

He felt the Peter and Paul Fortress buttressed at his back ; but life was naught to him.

And when it became known that Bobrov drank—it is easier to hide a thing from all-seeing God than from other people—and, moreover, became known that Bobrov drank alone, locked in, secretly, on the sly, this not only did not excite sympathy for him, no, this cut him off still more from the world.

It would have been another thing if he had drunk *in company*,—then he would have been one of themselves.

III

THE LIFE OF SILENCE

IF you ask for a glass of tea in Petersburg they will give you a glass, if you ask in Moscow they will give you a teapot, if you ask in Kiev take your own teapot, but if you ask in Stoudenets they will put a whole samovar on your table and glasses too,

With my treasure I part to the pleasure of my heart,—
something like that the proverb has it.

Stoudenets is situated on a hill; it is a wooded district.

Opposite the town on the other hill is a monastery. Once upon a time old hermit men labouring for God and the Church of God lived in it, recluses feeding on garlic and cutting the marsh hay in thoughts of God and in wise prayer, whereas now it is a nunnery and the nuns dry frog-roes and help women in childbirth and have introduced cows and take the milk for sale to the Lykov dairy ;—it is the Nunnery of Tikhvin.

Between the hills is a river, the *lumber* River Bear. Woods all round. In the woods there is a kind of ant and none fatter anywhere and the women catch them.

Scattered wooden houses ; palisading. Behind the hewn palisading scattered bushes, some sort of white willows, scraggy twigs alone sticking out. On palisadings suitable for relieving oneself verses scratched and chalked,—extremely edifying, though quite unsuitable for loud reading !

Cottages with overhanging eaves, all painted in most unexpected colours ; the whole village very bright.

Nakhabin's lonely stone house with gold lions at the gates—Nakhabin lives in style ; Oparin's three-storied hostelry ; and that red-brick packing-case Babashkov's flats ; a white stone church and a white stone prison.

The streets unpaved, a swamp between pavement and pavement. You cross the street on planks. The planks from age give way in the middle, and just look out in the Autumn—be sure you put on your goloshes or you will draw deep.

In the hollows are pools ; beside each house a kitchen garden. The pools are surrounded by cows and horses, and the gardens smell particularly well in the Spring of springtide town waterings. In the pools the Stoudenets pigs sleep like the dead and only some young sucker can be seen stirring up to its ears in slimy mud.

The town life moves nor turgid nor tripping from new year to new year, the New Year being met twice at a time, both on Saint Basil's Eve as it should be and on Saint Anysia's Day on the Thirtieth of December when every one meets it on his own account, as if an extra day of life had been granted.

Pens scratch away in the offices and typewriters rattle. When there is a fire the tocsin is sounded.

Practical jokers practical-joke ; they stick most unsuitable things made by folding from blue office paper (in the same way as paper boats) on Bobrov's window, or they smear the bell-pull with oil paint or they commit a nuisance on the doorstep or send a large registered parcel containing a beetroot or something that shape, well, say, to the girl Teacher Miss Fevral who puts by weekly scrapings from her salary in order to go to Petersburg and study.

In Summer when the ladies go down to the river to bathe, admirers hide in the bushes. No one can swim, but they splash about at the bank and scream, and only the wife of Bobrov the E.M. swims out to the centre.

Times and dates are registered in the peculiar Stoudenets reckoning system. For greater accuracy you are not told the year or the day, but the chronicable event worthy of remembrance.

' The same year,' people say, ' that the late County Judge Ivan Mikhailovitch Zakoutin broke Boudayev the Lawyer's windows.'

Or else : ' The same year that the Cemetery Parson the Rev. Azboukov together with his sister-in-law double-besomed his wife in the baths and became a member of the Consistorial Council.'

Or else : ' That very same year when Propenyshev's eldest daughter Iraida threw herself out of the window—I 'll fly, she said, to God—and broke herself to death.'

In Stoudenets for the weather too there is a special barometer.

The lunatics are kept on the upper floor of the prefecture ; if they sing, the weather will *change* ; if they yell, expect *rough* with *snow or rain* ; if they behave themselves, it is *set fair*.

In Winter there is a lot of snow, and hard frosts.

In Summer dust and scorching heat and mosquitoes.

In August you have to begin fires.

When the sun screws up its tipsy yellow eye behind two heavy pancake clouds, and sets behind the crumbling palisadings, and shutters are put up on the houses, and the whole town is already on its side,—alone the windows of the club show bright.

The Stoudenets Social Club is a place of *blind repose* and *wild perdition*.

There are five rooms in the club. In all five rooms the same walnuttish yellow wallpaper and a painted floor. Along the settee in the sitting-room there are greasy head patches ; seal of the conscientious labours of the Stoudenets hairdresser Youlin called Grishka Otrepyev. In the red corner a well-sat-in armchair, and from time immemorial the upholstering has been sliced by a knife. Hanging lamps with dangling glasses. A tobacco-boozy fug

The club library is next to the closets. ' Go

46

along to the library ' signifies ' I am going to the rears.'

Then, in the closet department itself, among all sorts of unprintable *wall verse* and rhetorical inscriptions, is drawn an historic phrase that comes from the Days of the Liberties, ' Long Live the Republic ! '

In the Winter the club subscribes to newspapers, in Summer it does not ; no one wants to read in the heat, so why ?

The club parlour-maid is all in pink with curls, the *Wassail Bowl* ; that is what the friends of the club call her, the *Wassail Bowl*.

The club cook Vassily is famous both for victuals and for drinks and unequalled for his ices ; people used to say, by the way, that Vassily put, and you would never have thought it, finely pulverized pepper into the ices.

The club barman Yermolai Ignatitch, one time in the Far East, could inimitably quack like a duck and rumble like a train, and keeps all the hors-d'œuvres under a meat-safe, not so much against the flies—who heard of flies in Winter !—but so that no one should, er, catching hold of something, er, carry it off.

The oldest clubman, District Member of the Court Ivan Feoktistovitch Bogoyavlensky, is lame, and he drinks and there is not much that 'scapes his eye, and he never leaves the club without some winnings. and though for that matter he has never been caught you would really think he was a cheat.

The members of the club are all birds of a feather.

Alexander Ilitch, the Police Captain and no other, is the first member.

After him come the Stoudenets ranks like this :

The Town Judge Nalimov, Stepan Stepanitch, sober as a cock, and only once a year, on his birthday, does he level up with Ivan Nikanoritch Toroptsov, and the doctor likes to boast that he once sat through nineteen bottles in one evening ;

the Local Government Board Officer Saltanovsky Nicholas Vassilievitch, *the Law-worm* ;

the Excise Officer Shverin, Sergey Sergeitch, the sportsman of Stoudenets. You can tell him in any brawl you like by his university badge of enormous proportions, and he is a dabster at telling of foreign ways and means, and they call him *Table d'hôte* or *Maître d'hôtel*, which comes more fitting ;

Pratkin, Semyon Fyodorovitch, the Agricultural Expert, after twelve introduces himself as the *Svinya*, or hog, is extraordinarily sensitive and given to weeping and can sob like any Dove of Spring ; and his friends tease him about Agrafena whom he married to hide the misdeed of another, though how this came about he never can remember ;

the Secretary of the L.G.B. Vassily Petrovitch Nyemov, a clever fellow with more sense than any of the others, but when a wave overtakes him he sits for weeks on end in the club drinking it with bitters ;

the Tax-collector Stroisky, Vladimir Nikolaievitch, the Stoudenets *Don Juan*; in his cups clinging as Doctor Toroptsov; just out of them, weeps like the Agricultural Expert Pratkin;

the Postmaster, Arkady Pavlovitch Yarlykov, the huntsman of Stoudenets, his quiver full like that of the Surveyor Karinsky;

the Forester Kourganovsky, Erast Evgrafovitch, called *the Water-trough*;

Member of the L.G.B. Semyon Mikheitch Rogatkin, a contractor, supplier of hay and timber, even builds bridges, a man of the people, does not so much drink as ply others; and

the immutable Grokhotov, Peter Petrovitch, the Veterinary Surgeon, called *the Bird of Paradise*, goes about in the cold season with no coat on, quick of foot, and although a family man (every one knows his old woman), he is as homeless as Poppá Paul, the vagabond of Stoudenets, and bent of limb, and sleeps sprawled where the fumes take him; then, after Petrousha,

all sorts, Teachers and Clerks and Divers other Scriveners.

The most active of the club ladies is the wife of the Captain of Police, Maria Severyanovna.

After Maria Severyanovna follow her friends:

Anna Savinovna, wife of the Excise Officer, head of a school of needlework;

the wife of the E.M., Prascovia Ivanovna; and the wife of Dr. Toroptsov, Katerina Vladimirovna,

49

the songstress of Stoudenets, known with sly meaning as *Country Kate*, and although she has never been further than Kazan she can turn a conversation with any one travelled, as if she had lived just out of Petersburg all her life.

In the club they play cards, eat, converse. They play Loo and Preference, Whist rarely enough, and, after twelve, Chemin de fer. Conversation consists of Stoudenets intrigues, no one has an opinion about anything,—as the wind blows.

' Times, you know, have changed,' that is the favourite refrain, after which expect a response exactly the opposite of yesterday's.

At one o'clock every one goes home; it doesn't do to go too far.

The road from the club goes past the house of the Chairman of the L.G.B., Byelozerov; feet unsteady, but withal well-accustomed, traditionally lead to the house of the Chairman. The Chairman Byelozerov is the Stoudenets Squire, a dandy with a *finishing-off* in a high school at his back, who held aloof from the club group—but the point was not in Byelozerov himself, but in his *Vassilisa the Fair*.

This Vassilisa the Fair the Chairman had plucked for himself,—straight from the root, as Istsov-Pelican put it; Vassilisa worked at the pump on a barge, and Byelozerov saw her and his eyes rested on Vassilisa and his heart leapt and he purchased her from her parents.

Byelozerov kept Vassilisa locked in his house,

watched like a vulture over the white body and only on holy days, attired to the pitch of fashion, did he release her to attend communion at the church. And God only knows for what purpose,—now, was it simply from *unsociability* ?—he used to make Vassilisa strip and walk about like that, naked, in the drawing-room hung round with mirrors, and he would stretch himself out on the sofa and lie there and smoke ; or he would make her dust the floor, which in any case was polished like a mirror, and he would again lie and watch.

Through the crack in the lighted window you can see it all ; there 's no need to screw your eye up.

And in the hour of deep Stoudenets slumber, in the hour of the second cock-crow, you can often see the midnight friends close to the window, close to the crack in Byelozerov's lighted window, and there comes a point when Petrousha Grokhotov tears at the wall with his nails.

Further on, the road turns towards the house of the E.M., Bobrov. The friends do not let him off either, and without fail some one's fist bangs on the shutters.

But in the upper window of the magistrate's house a lonely sleepless light burns steadily away and makes no stir.

*

Ever since his family ceased to be, his home was destroyed, alone evening to evening in a life of silence, Bobrov consecrated a large portion of the hours of night to writing besides reading.

His book was rather curious, something like a Bill of Accusation, not of some unknown individual, not of an accused criminal of Stoudenets, but of the whole Russian people ; and it was like Ivan Timofeyev the Clerk in ancient days, in the Troublous Times, in his Chronicle, pronouncing his condemnation of the Russian people, ' *who were silent and spake not !* '

The Monk of the Trinity too, Avramy Palitsin, condemned the Russian people, ' *for its insensate silence.*'

From the foundations of Moscow, from the commencement of the Russian Kingdom down to the last disturbance—the memorable Days of the Liberties—Bobrov was assembling the deeds of the nation and pronouncing his judgment on them.

Outrages, oppression, destruction, straitness, want, pillage, treachery, murder, disorder, and lawlessness, that is *the Russian land*.

Shifting, disunited, by a thousand deliriums divided, erratic and silent, voiceless, that is *the Russian people*.

Bobrov turned to the conscience of the Russian people, because in the conscience of the people is the peace of this earth.

What can save the Russian land, divided, burned away, broken, crushed and desolated ? What can end rebellion ? What destroy injustice ? What quench hatreds ? And where is the Rod of the emperor ?

All cast to the winds, all brought to destruction !

Where upright and fearless thoughts, where the unflinching heart ? They think they are ruling and building, but they lead the country to evil things ! Disorder will bring low the Kingdom of Russia and disorder sweep away the Russian people. The Law, this thing from all time unknown to Russia, this is the pillar on which a nation can be built.

In time the work was thrown aside, he had no more mind to write, but all his energy, all his inspiration, the feeling that penetrated every word, insolently, commandingly addressed to the people of Russia, to his own country, made sense in that senseless broken life of Bobrov. He knew the purpose of his rising every morning and going down to his small examining office and sitting there patiently till evening, worming things out and signing forms, and during the hunt in inquiries racing hound-like over the tracks of the criminal.

Law, the sole salvation of Russia on her path to destruction ;

Law, to outroot that root, the duty of every Russian that loved his motherland ;

Law, without which no Russian Kingdom can ever be ;

Law, which he in his deeds furthered ;

which was his fortress, the sense of his life—the *labour of his soul*.

The book lay in a drawer of his writing-desk, the drawer under lock and key. And months passed, years, and he did not open that book, but in minutes of madness in the lonely night all his thoughts were turned to the sacred manuscript, to the cross of his labours; and his rage burned furiously. Seated before the mirror alone in the midst of night, by night he would hold his secret converse, fiery speech, —to the mirror, to himself,—as if from the Trafalgar Square of Moscow, the Lobnoie Mesto, or from the Peter Plinth, from the base of the Petersburg monument to the Great Russian Emperor, he spake to the people of Russia.

That pain, that stifling misery of his own ruination that made the very air dense, and bred desire to drink to stupefaction, poured out in the course of years in most scathing accusations, in a lament over the ruination of the Russian lands, the destruction of the Russian people. And it seemed that in his hand he held the power that would unite and resolve, seemed that he knew the root of the evil, the means of salvation, and could show what would save Russia and how.

And every day life, senseless, brought fresh lawlessnesses to him.

' Then has this anarchic violence perhaps entered into the blood and body of the Russian people,' he

asked himself, 'and all are confounded, and the
Russia built up through the centuries is falling to
ruins and will crumble away and the last Russian will
forget his own speech, while death sleeps not—and
a powerful foreign people will swarm in hordes over
the land, death sleeping not, and distracted, broken,
weakened, spat upon, foreign lips spitting, own lips
spitting, the Russian people, besotted, the *ne'er-do-
well* people, will without fight, nay, brother betraying
brother on its ruined fields, yield to the enemy.'

'The day will come,' he used to say, 'yes, it is
true, the prophecy is true, the days are already
nigh, the hour approaching, when those that dwell
in this house will no more walk within it and its
gates will be closed and never more opened, and
this house will be desolate, Russia will be desolate.'
While before his eyes from the darkness of centuries
rose up that Russia that was built in those days
when cathedrals were erected and the joists of
wooden churches mortised and the bells hung in
the bell-towers. A great fire destroys everything,
to the very last stone, and then again persistently,
patiently, stones are brought to the cindery ground
and timber, and anew the building raised ; thus town
by town did the people lay the foundation to a great
Kingdom, Russia. And the stronger the Church, the
higher the Temple, the louder ring the bells, the
stronger is the town, the bolder speech, Russian
speech ; and thus temple by temple was Russia built.

Then, behold, not Akhmylla the pagan accursed,

but a terrible Tsar comes to his land and destroys
his own Russian town, what time the Metropolitan
of Novgorod decked as a clown was led on a white
mare about the town with cap and bells by the
command of the Tsar ; what time publicly full half
a thousand monks put to torture were beaten to
death with rods ; then, even thus early lawlessness
entered as poison Russian blood ! And the Saint
of Moscow, the martyr, the faithful and firm-
couraged son of Russia, was right, saying :

> ' the Tartars have their justice, only Russia
> has none; in the whole world you will
> find mercy, but in Russia there is no feel-
> ing or mercy even for the innocent or just '

And one after another, chastisement of death
after chastisement of death, mortal to the nation—
lawlessness, wild destruction from above ; more
ruinous still destruction and pogrom from below,—
the chain of centuries rose up before him in ever
increasing fury, Moscow and her torture-chambers,
the Troublous Times and treachery, and Petersburg
and its crime, all to the last disturbance, the memorable Days of the Liberties.

Lawless, blood-bespattered, debauched in lawlessness, the Russian people began to seem to him
a dog-headed people *imprisoned*, that, at the end of
all time, in the last day of this world and of light,
was to cast itself, squirming with howls and intoxicated by liberation from its thousand-year

confinement, upon the peoples of liberty and annihilate all kingdoms.

The lawless deeds of his own people were set in vermin, and its lips seethed in blood.

When in a peasant pogrom the peasants gouged out the horses' eyes after firing the manor house ;

when in a Jewish pogrom the hooligans drove nails into victims' eyes and skulls ;

when the warder in a police-station put out his cigarette-end on an arrested woman's naked body ;

when street-robbers who had robbed a passer-by cut off his lip—well, just for something to do ;

when revolutionaries kill right and left on the simple order of a provocator ;

when thieves crucified a merchant by nailing his hands to the wall and his feet to the floor, in order to extort money ;

when judges publicly approve an admitted pogrom-murderer ;

whose are these acts, what people's ?

And he remembered how, recently, some hooligans had dealt in cold blood with a sectarian because he refused to cross himself, had poured water over him and thrashed him, while policemen looked on from the window and encouraged them ; and they, exasperated by his patience, then threw him on his face on the floor and some sat on his back while the rest *twisted the duck* to break his neck, but did not break it, and then stuffed up his nose and mouth with tobacco ; whose is this act, what people's ?

And when the village lads out for a game met the parson and made him dance ;

when at a wedding a contractor undertook to show a workman how to teach his wife, and beat this other man's pregnant wife with a leather saddle-girth ;

when a horse-stealer had a pole thrust up his anus ;

when a mother puts her daughter on the rails and orders her to throw herself under the train, ' lie you down there, you 're no use to any one ! '

and another mother finds a purchaser ;

when in a provincial court putting accused persons to the question, one was burned with a red-hot iron, another strung up and the soles of his feet roasted, a third had oil poured on his back and fired, a fourth fine-cut horsehair thrust up his penis ;

whose are these acts, what dissipated people's, the soul in it killed ;

what treacherous head, treacherous to its motherland, conceived such deeds to the perdition of itself and the nation ? And the sniggering cowardly public with its monkey laughter doing nothing . . . sluggards and parasites, thieves desirous of concealing their idleness, shouting their cheap pogrom warcry at the street-corners and seeing in this low hunting the task of Russia ; the poor of soul, blind idiot-monsters, the beggarly of spirit, who find nothing else for Russia's civilization, for the people of Russia, but to desecrate and accurse Russia !

A *job* ye have found, a task for Russia ye have found!

Hypocritical prostitutable authorities, thrusting the law on others, yourselves breaking it, you the first bewrayers, the first traitors, the first criminals!

Abject public, abject people!

To whom is Russia dear?

Who is faithful to her?

Who cares for her?

Who keeps his oath to serve her faithfully, immutably, inseparably . . . no,

No Russian be I! and Bobrov would revolt from the mirror,

No Russian, a German! all Russians traitors and thieves!

And he stood there alone, to himself alone,—the refalling stone—alone, his fist raised before the whole people, while his rod, his staff,—*the Law*—the death-dealing symbol, descended like a cross erect quietly upon the earth. And with him the whole Russian people buried itself away in gloom, shifting, disunited, silent.

Consciousness, dying, gave one flicker more; despair was laying waste his soul, and to the sound of hammering on the shutter by the gay club friends homeward bound Bobrov fell rolling there, senseless, mindless, and the sleep of fumes, dreamless sleep, heavy and terrible, covered with dark blood, crushed and enwound him till senseless morning, till the day of work.

IV

HEARTS AND HEADS OF OAK

W<small>HETHER</small> our many and grievous sins and evil-doings, as the chronicler would say, were the cause, or we were quite innocent, and there were other causes having no connection whatsoever with sin, and, well, it was simply like that,—a multitude of most unexpected events came to pass in Stoudenets.

Last year the storekeeper of the *deoperative society*, Kotchnov, a former A.B., suddenly, for no apparent reason that we could see, in expectation of the coming comet fastened himself to an anchor and dug himself into the ground.

It was only with Petrousha Grokhotov's help, so Petrousha assured the whole club, that Kotchnov was pulled out of his pit, but the poor fellow did not see much more of God's world and fell into a melancholy and expired before the arrival of the comet.

And this Spring, on all sides, worms appeared in Stoudenets in incalculable multitudes. The worms crawled over the slushy snow from the house of the Pharmaceutist Gleicher past Oparin's Inn, past Ponyoushkin the Paymaster, straight to the house of the Rural Dean Vinogradov,—widdershins.

And they multiplied with lightning-like celerity, as Petrousha said.

Three days and three nights the worms crawled

towards the Rural Dean, and then of a sudden turned on the Police Captain and disappeared.

And while they were crawling the weather was warm, but when they disappeared it became windy.

Nobody ventured to touch the maggots, and even the Prison Governor Vedyornikov, goodness alone knows how much more famed than any other person for such deeds, he was crazy about cleanliness—for cleanliness' sake he kept the prisoners naked in their cells—even he did not put a finger to them.

But the creatures, though in outward appearance bearing a similitude to worms, still there was *a message* in 'their bodily composition and in the dissection of their nature,' all covered with little scattered hairs, and some had little wriggling legs like teats on the belly, while the belly of others was quite smooth.

The widowed wife of the Deacon Agntsev, a responsible member of the *deoperative society*, she caught a pair and then used to exhibit them in the shop to all persons desirous.

But the creatures, though in outward appearance bearing a similitude to worms . . . —but that was a trifle, and bore no similitude whatever to the event that took place the morning after the celebration of the Rural Dean's Saint's Day.

' But once in a blue moon such a thing,' was the talk that evening in the club when they all came to.

Ass's ears sprang up on the Stoudencts Police Captain, Alexander Ilitch, in miraculous manner.

And this not in any figurative sense, but in actual fact, in all veritability, and moreover in only one night—and what is a night! in those few hours, who knows, in fact, perhaps in a single minute, unexpectedly, suddenly they sprang up, ears like this, above his heavy short-cropped brow, and waved in the air in most unseeming fashion.

Of course, on another man—heaven knows there are enough kinds of physiognomy in the world, why yes, and here, on the spot, in Stoudenets, there are enough of them, if you only take that afore-mentioned Lepetov the Diocesan Superintendent or the Member of the Diocesan Council, also a Lepetov, the provincial one who comes into Stoudenets for the examinations as examiner, and better known as the *Pickled Cucumberkin*—why, those ears would quite suit these, and, who knows, might have made real men of them.

But Alexander Ilitch was not Lepetov the Superintendent, was not Lepetov the Examiner, the *Pickled Cucumberkin*, and such an acquisition was the last straw for Alexander Ilitch, a divine scourge, a most unseeming thing.

With all his dashing harmony of style—and he can inspire and he can terrify—well, were it a pair of antlers, they might work in not too badly, but even then, you are quite right, not really satisfactorily when you think of the silver in his beard and the old man's short wind; yes, with all his real dignity and radiance, and the Stoudenets Police

Captain was known as *Old Sunbeam,*—suddenly crowning all, those awful ears !

The Dean, the Rev. Nicholas Vinogradov, has only one birthday—that is, Saint's Day,—in a year, but it is good for the whole twelve months.

The table would be well laden, there would be no empty plate, and

Ye lamb went round with egge-balls flourished

as the celebrator said—a leg of mutton roasted with force-meat.

And all that was lacking were struthocamelian eggs ; and they plied the bottle, some stonily labouring though fallen, others labouring fallen like stones.

At the party of the year before last the late Mayor Taldykin met death by the judgment of the Lord ; he failed to maintain the struggle and rendered his soul to God.

Alexander Ilitch feasted at the parson's house, and sin was committed, the parson seducing him with *ruddy fructificated mead,* after which followed wine good and foamy, and Alexander Ilitch let himself go and failed to observe his Holy-Rood Day oath.

But nothing in particular took place ; at cards he had better luck than ever before and he beat everybody else and raked in a pile of gold, too much for his pockets, and he went home on both feet.

But then in the morning, *from sleep experging,* as the dean celebrating would have said, and smoothing his sturdy hedgehog head, Alexander Ilitch with a shudder felt on himself the presence of improper objects ; and he immediately in some way realised the situation and understood that these were not his own ears, that on him were *ass's ears*, and that they were very firmly attached.

The wife of the E.M., Prascovia Ivanovna Bobrov, dreams about bulls, bull on bull and all chasing her, trying to catch her ;

the Postmaster, Arkady Pavlovitch Yarlykov, the huntsman, in his sleep sees ducks and geese and all species of wildfowl ;

the Forester Kourganovsky does not dream at all ; while .

the Police Captain, although he does not often dream, sees night after night, if a dream does come, military engagements.

But Alexander Ilitch felt those ears, not in dream, but waking ; and it appears that, aware of what had happened, for long he could not summon courage to go up to the mirror and look ; and sat on the sofa (they had made his bed on the sofa away from his wife), and he sat there and felt himself, that is, his ears. He would get hold of the lobe and twist it round his skull and give it wrench enough to rend it out.

And the more he twisted and turned them the stronger he felt them to be, and without any of your mirrors he could see himself there as clear as ever was, his fine Antonovian stature and his radiance ; the Anne medal at his neck, the ribbons on his breast, his wonderful tan, his winged beard, hair combed to hair ; and, God alone knows, there, full two fingers long, oily, with a sort of yellowish tint, sticking up from through the sparse hair that resembled that of the widowed-wife-of-the-Deacon-Agntsev's maggots—stuck up the ass's ears.

The C.P. in Stoudenets is like the Governor in a provincial capital such as Lykov, he is the highest of all ; can make rich and make poor, humiliate and elevate. And of course, if he presented himself, well, say in the church, at some service, and, say, in the shape of a dog, that afore-mentioned Vinogradov would still bring him the cross first.

Alas, alas, that it was ears,

> *and of its strength the scythe shall*
> *mow down every man !*

The books of time are memorable—and the chronicles of Stoudenets record events out and out more remarkable and such things were not done and performed,

> *and there was peace and love, order and decency.*

Nobody dared to laugh at the C.P.

Gobbet-Bobrov—Bobrov came into the C.P.'s mind, and the mere recollection of the Examining Magistrate threw him into a heat. And Alexander Ilitch counted over everybody, all the inhabitants of Stoudenets from the Chairman of the L.G.B. Byelozerov down to the Beggar-Page and Florry the Whore.

And he went through all the club company, the

senior of the club, Member of the Court Bogoyav-
lensky, and the Judge Nalimov, and the L.G.B.
Officer Saltanovsky-Law worm, and the Exciseman
Shverin Table-d'hôte and the L.G.B. Secretary
Nyemov and the Agriculturist Pratkin the Hog,
and the Tax-collector Stroisky Don Juan, and the
Postmaster Arkady Pavlovitch Yarlykov, and the
Surveyor Karinsky, and Toroptsov the Police Doctor,
and the Forester Kourganovsky the Water-Trough,
and he doubted not in any one of them.

Bobrov, Bobrov the E.M., he alone for ever came
into his head.

Verily, verily, the Lord is yielding, Satan active.

Bobrov would not be inquisitive like the other, or
ask out of friendship, ' I say, where did you get
that ? God's mercy, and who did it ? ' but on the
other hand he would give such a stare, though
most likely avoid him just as one avoids excre-
ment, so as not to tread in it ; and then, another
fine thing, those ears—insult to injury !—would start
twitching.

' Would his ears twitch or not ? ' now became the
question, and Alexander Ilitch's spirits fell. And
everything swam greenish before his eyes, and fiery
match-sticks danced ; and he felt how, at the thought
of it alone, the ears twitched of their own accord
and set hopping up and down like a horse's.

If only his wife Maria Severyanovna had been at
home the matter would have been put to rights
somehow,—Maria Severyanovna would put any-

thing right. But his wife was at the *Devil's Gardens*; she had work enough there without those ears.

And what would he say to Maria Severyanovna?

He had broken his Holy-Rood oath, he had not kept his word.

What sort of an answer would he give Maria Severyanovna?

She would not thank him; and that a lot, too; and it would have been better for him not to have wakened at all after the Dean's birthday celebration, and thus in sleep repose *till that joyous dawning*.

'Why has this happened to me? So cruel! If it had been a mortal sin, for fornication with birds or for belly-ripping, but all I did was drink a little glass of wine at a Saint's Day celebration at the parson's, at the Rural Dean's, a spiritual father,— moreover drank to his health and many returns. Yes, yes, I broke my oath, I did not keep my promise, I made a mistake, I do not resist.' Alexander Ilitch sat on the sofa and twitched his ears.

'Maria Severyanovna, thou hast not left me?' ran his bitter thoughts. 'Maria Severyanovna, leave me not!'

In prayer Alexander Ilitch raised his eyes:

'Leave me not!'

And suddenly, not believing his eyes, he began wildly rocking his head; straight in front of him, under his famous cross-wove carpet of various foreign beasts with the hair of twelve various species of wolf about which people said it was priceless, and worth ' God knows how many millions and hordillions of untold money '—the gift of the Nuns of Tikhvin—under this priceless carpet on the sofa like a corpse lay Petrousha Grokhotov.

' Petrousha ! ' Alexander Ilitch called out, ' Pyotitchka ! '

And his breathing grew silent, his heart thudded, as in childhood at big houses on fire, of which Alexander Ilitch had always been a great lover. All his hope was in Petrousha the *Veterinary*.

To a shout Petrousha was sharp as a horse, however deep his sleep ; even through his corpsical tipsy oblivion he heard the shout, and he spat out and he spat down in the pure Russian manner ; (and by nature free of any nervousness of speech or movement, even in the presence of ladies Petrousha swore,—only then in the Little Russian dialect).

' Petrousha, Pyotitchka ! '

Alexander Ilitch could not recognize his own voice : it was like the fox's squeak when he seduced the cock with the green peas, and in real life Alexander Ilitch did not talk like that, even as Lykov Police Captain to Lykov Province Governor. His ears were twitching mercilessly and he pulled them up tightly over his crown ; ' Save me, Petrousha ! ' he cried.

Petrousha rose up and his vodka-oiled eye fixed itself on the Police Captain—Petrousha's hair standing like that of a devil in arrows upwards—and Petrousha's *cannon* suddenly burst forth with such a cloud of smoke that the bright May morning was darkened and the C.P. sailed away with his ears in some unknown direction.

Tearfully Alexander Ilitch told his affliction to his friend. ' Hoof ointment,' said Petrousha, without waiting for all of it, ' the cracks in hoofs heal from it, excellent remedy ! ' And all that remained was for Petrousha to apply his infallible remedy at once, Alexander Ilitch being ready not only to smear this ointment on, but even to take it internally, as much as his body would hold, if only it would have some effect. But Petrousha suddenly spun round like a bird on a spit and burst into song really like a Bird of Paradise.

About such a thing happening once before, not just to an *anybody*, not to a common fellow, but to a king ; ass's ears had grown out on the head of the *Phrygian King*—Alexander Ilitch had absolutely no knowledge, no idea of this—but Petrousha did remember something or other, though it is true he mixed up Midas with the great namesake of the C.P.

But the ancient story of Noah, how Noah the Righteous bridled the wild beasts in the Ark, Alexander Ilitch knew as well as Petrousha.

There is a story of Noah, how Noah the Righteous, when he had let the beasts into the ark, seven pairs of the clean and two pairs each of the unclean, had the brilliant idea of bridling them, and, for general comfort, of depriving them (temporarily, of course) of most necessary *appurtenances* ; and, confiscating these treasures of each with great solicitude he placed them in a shrine, in a hidden place.

And forty days and forty nights, the whole period of the flood, the beasts sat peacefully in their cages.

When the flood was over and the shrine was opened the beasts rushed at their *acquirements* and each sorted out his own. And it was only in the case of the elephant that there was a great confusion, to the embitterment of that animal and the rejoicement and pride of the ass; for the elephant got the ass's and the ass the elephant's.

The ass getting hold of the elephant's portion and the Phrygian King with the ass's ears excited Petrousha's imagination. And it is true enough that Petrousha earned his daily bread with his tongue, not his hands.

Alexander Ilitch, he said, would get into *Greek History* and in the high schools they would *translate him* from the Greek and get bad marks and fail in their examinations; and it goes without saying that he would get an increase, practically become a Governor, and get to Petersburg and a Ministerial Portfolio guaranteed

Minister of Public Education !

' With such a golden treasure,' like a Bird of Paradise poured forth Petrousha, ' why, with fire you would find no such other, with no oak cudgelling acquire, *a historical fact*, Cabinet Minister ! Look at him and learn ! And our ladies ! There 'll be no resistance, you can cuckold Byelozerov. We 'll

show him the three fingers, you 'll have the Fair
Vassilisa wiping the floor for you.'

Alexander Ilitch wanted promotion very much,
but what promotion had to do with his plight he
could not make out. As for the ladies, and however
seductive the idea might be that Vassilisa the Fair
would wipe the floor for him, Alexander Ilitch tried
to turn a deaf ear to it all. Alexander Ilitch had
once got into great difficulties through the ladies.
When he was Policemaster of Lykov Alexander
Ilitch gave permission to some circus dancers to
ride their bicycles through Lykov down the Moscow
Road in full daylight in all their beautiful *birthday
dresses*; and they did do it. The naked dancers
rode down the street, but he flew from his job.

The hoof ointment in which Alexander Ilitch
believed, and which he kept firmly in mind, cooled
all Petrousha's temptation. Petrousha was building
such phantasy, painting such consequences, and
there was no bottom to the sea of his words.

'Why, with such a head a bed of oak, you bloody
fool, that 's no common or garden thing, you know.
Did you ever see such on an ass ? Anybody you
like you can cork up ! The world lies before you ! '

'Petrousha, have mercy,' the C.P., unable to
bear any more, interrupted him ; ' Pyotitchka, get
your hoof ointment.'

'*Hoof ointment*,' Petrousha mocked him, ' —he
runs from his own good fortune ! '

And, grunting out something really very unsuitable, he began to dress, and was soon quite ready, buttoned up and pulled straight, and only had to put his cap on his head and pass the door.

' Petrousha,' Alexander Ilitch's voice even shook, ' please, please, on your word, don't tell any one ! '

' All right, sit still ! '   And he fluttered away.

And while Petrousha was flying for his most miraculous hoof ointment to his benefactor the Chemist Adolf Franz Gleicher, and while he was there and all this went on, an event happened in Stoudenets worthy of no small amazement and even of tears.

*

Stoudenets is a trading town.

Nakhabin, Tabouryaiev, Propenyshev, Zatchessov, timber-merchants, and the District Member of the Court Bogoyavlensky trade through Istsov-Pelican the scribe.

The feverish time is the winter, the place bubbles with work ; the winter preparations for the coming floating down, lumber being got to the river.   And the timber-yards grow with every floating.

Stoudenets is a town with means ; and the telegraph is not inactive one day in the year ; no sitting with folded arms there.   Nyousha Kroutikov, the telegraph girl, was always receiving the same things for Nakhabin, for Tabouryaiev, for Yarlykov, for Propenyshev and for Zatchessov, and could see no prospect of a change.

But besides these business telegrams there were chance ones to the L.G.B. Chairman Byelozerov, to the Prison Governor Vedyornikov, to the Marshal of Nobility Babakhin, and two delayed telegrams to the Rural Dean the Rev. Vinogradov :

' HAPPIEST RETURNS OF THE DAY '; and one, simply, as Wildboar Vasya said, ' like any petticoat would write ' :

' GOD BLESS YOU ON YOUR BIRTHDAY ! '

Wildboar Vasya

sold the stamps.

It was market day, and people kept coming into the post office, and a number were waiting there. The day promised to be hot, and there was a proper post-office fug on.

Nyousha Kroutikov suddenly brightened up ; something interesting lay on the tape, a telegram, a telegram to Stoudenets, and what a telegram !

The telegram was addressed to Lepetov the Diocesan Superintendent :

STOUDENETS ELEVEN AM MOTORCAR
GOVERNOR ARRIVING

And the first person to learn of this piece of news was Wildboar Vasya. Immediately, not wasting one second, Yeremey the porter took this telegram out of turn to Lepetov the Superintendent. By which time the whole post office knew about the Governor. And those who were jostling there, hands full of parcels, speedily spread the news about the market.

Wildboar Vasya ran bareheaded to tell the Post-master, Arkady Pavlovitch. Arkady Pavlovitch, as the other dignitaries of Stoudenets, was in peaceful slumber after the parson's birthday party; and dreamed of his well-loved wildfowl.

Arkady Pavlovitch dreamed he was sitting on the roof of his fowlhouse with Mrs. Baretkin the mid-wife, and geese were flying by, a whole flight right over their heads. And Arkady Pavlovitch said to his fair neighbour:

'I say, Agrafena Ivanovna, let 's have 'em!'

And one goose separated from the rest and flew towards the fowlhouse, and they stretched forth their hands and beckoned to it, wanted to catch it; when suddenly it flew extra-ordinarily quickly and unnoticeably at Arkady Pavlovitch and pecked him straight in the palm; whereupon Arkady Pavlovitch snatched the goose, pafff! by the neck, and there, it wasn't a goose at all, but a hawk, and such a hawk. . . .

Wildboar Vasya, dribbling and lisping both as a normal function and from his excitement, trans-mitted the news of tremendous character to forcibly awakened Arkady Pavlovitch; he himself, Wildboar Vasya, and he had received the telegram at twenty-three minutes to ten.

Without washing, without drinking tea, Arkady Pavlovitch wrenched on his uniform and ran, ran straight to the Police Captain. And his shaggy three-legged white bitch Oscar rushed off after him.

'The Governor himself—in a motor car!' It bumped so on the potholes the Postmaster went alternately hot and cold.

Alexander Ilitch was sitting on his sofa ; and over him laboured Petrousha, who had found time to let more than one slip down for the lubrication of his voice at his benefactor's the Chemist Gleicher's. The Vet. was rubbing the C.P.'s ears with something fiery, some sort of vernigrease, touching, for his own amusement or in his eagerness, upon parts that had no concern whatever in the matter, first slapping on to his nose, then smearing all over his neck. And this was the very hoof ointment in which Alexander Ilitch longed to believe.

Tears flowed in streams from his eyes, damping his purple cheeks, yet patiently he bore his bitter pains, though vainly, for 'tis little likely such agonies be credited him in the next world.

The Postmaster observed neither the unusual ears nor the bitter tears—nothing of that. Without any good-day he burst forth about the Governor, addressing himself not so much to the C.P. as to the cross-wove carpet that cost so 'many thousand millions and hordillions of untold money,'

'at eleven o'clock the Governor is coming !' And as if by a hand-touch, better than the very hoof ointment, in one second the ears put themselves straight and from ass's ears became again Antonovian. Alexander Ilitch sprang up from the sofa, and, thus all smeared up, ran into the hall with the Postmaster.

And indeed in one minute all Stoudenets was brought to its feet.

All the four constables were despatched about the town.

The Mayor Oparin, the Rural Dean Vinogradov, the Military Commander Kobyrdyaiev, the L.G.B. Officer Saltanovsky, all had to be informed, and, what was more important, at all costs Maria Severyanovna recalled from the *Devil's Gardens*.

Everything was being cleaned, everything washed, everything scraped and anointed and sluiced and put straight and smoothed out and swept and squeezed back and strewn with sand.

And over everything through the atmosphere diffused our exquisite national swearing, of aid in all situations.

The little boys were being marched to the Deanery Church from the town school and the parish schools and the high school.

Shvedov the Teacher was arranging a parade of the Boys' Brigade.

The policemen were floundering here, there, everywhere, not knowing what to do. The dogs were running. The brood-hens were fluttering with great noise. People had lost their heads driving the pigs into their yards. The dust was whirling higher than the bell-tower of the church.

Absurdity, confusion, topsy-turvydom.

The crowd was collecting by the church for the reception.

The Military Commander Kobyrdyaiev arrived, a little old man who smelled of ointments,—tonquin-bean, camphor and opodeldoc.

And the Chairman of the L.G.B., alone, without Vassilisa the Fair.

And the Paymaster Ponyoushkin *the Grabber*, who went to law about a fox with the late Mayor Taldy-kin; and they took the thing to the Senate and wrote petitions to the Emperor, and the result was that when he had paid forty-five roubles costs Taldykin died, and the fox's skin, which had been handed to the police for safe keeping, rotted away.

The Judge Nalimov too was in his place;

and Bogoyavlensky the lame Member of the Court;

and the L.G.B. Officer Saltanovsky *Law-worm*;

and the Excise Officer Shverin *Table d'hôte*;

and the Agricultural Expert Pratkin *the Hog*;

and the Forester Kourganovsky the *Water-trough*;

and the Tax-collector *Don Juan*;

and the Prison Governor Vedyornikov, fussing about with his little eyes bulging from fear;

and Arkady Pavlovitch the Postmaster;

and the Rural Police Commissioner Lagoutin, all puffy with hairy fists ;

and Rogatkin, Member of the L.G.B. ;

and the afore-mentioned Stoudenets merchant world in their medals, Tabouryaiev, Yargounov, Propenyshev and Zatchessov ; all most superior personages in full parade.

Only the greatest of all was wanting, Nakhabin, absent on business in Lykov.

The Rural Dean the Rev. Nicholas Vinogradov came out with a cross, and took up his stand amid the assembly of Stoudenets clergy,

lord of the barnyard, *cockerel*, *cock*, PEACOCK.

And Alexander Ilitch, himself, the *Sunbeam*, with his cap jammed down over his ears, as indeed afterwards everybody tried to have been first to remark, —Alexander Ilitch himself in all his glory, terrible as a very lion, was dealing out orders, and all was done according to his word. While Alexander Ilitch's assistant Kopyev in his inseparable felt-slippers was chasing an obstinate cow,—however much they tried they could not get that cow off the Square.

And only the mayor, Paul Diévitch Oparin, was not to be seen. However much they tried to waken Oparin, his sleep remained undisturbable. . . . And all measures were taken that are taken in such cases ; the clang of bells and the bellow of trumpets ; that same indispensable Petrousha Grokhotov it was who laboured, but nothing could rouse the

Mayor. And they had fallen into real despair when the barman of the club, Yermolai Ignatytch, advised them to try

bug powder.

And bug powder brought Oparin into the light of God's day.

And they took the Mayor to the assembly and they placed him in position.

And there stood Oparin the Mayor, the symbolic dish of bread and salt swaying in his hands, in stupefaction.

The freakish supernumerary parson Pessotchensky, who inadvertently buried a dead man with three legs, one of them a gutta-percha one, pushed in most unsuited manner in a peaked cap like any pilgrim among the choristers who were clearing their throats.

The *plaguey* parson, the Rev. Landyshev, possessor of living and dead, stood in a smart new calotte by the banner of the League of Towns among the Stoudenets shopkeepers, who of old scorn Lykov sausages, believing that the meat is made with human flesh, one pound of human to two stone of pork.

Zavoulonsky the Deacon nosed about among the lads, and picking out the smallest whippersnappers, puffed in the brats' noses ; ' When I blow, can you smell it ? ' the Deacon was inquiring ; but what power could hide the Dean's last night birthday celebrations, moreover at such short notice !

The Chairman of the L.G.B., Byelozerov, who kept aloof from Stoudenets society, only frowned scornfully.

The market day had collected as many people as if it were a royal holiday. The whole town was full, rows of them past the church to the very bridge, and already you could only elbow your way through, and that with difficulty.

Even old Shapaiev, that *heals by fornication*, never quitting his garden, stood blinking from the sun in a circle of peasant-women disciples (women faithful and God-fearing, or, as they described themselves, *God-militant*), capless, mournful, an icon on his breast.

And old Mother Spinnilegs—surnamed Philipiev, omnipresent, span about, driven from place to place, alone, without her faithful Gennashka, who had stayed behind to look after *The Kolpaks*. And Istsov the Pelican and Youlin the Barber, Grishka Otrepyev. And old Poppá Paul the Vagabond beating round, shamelessly worming out his *page's portion*.

The urchins clung round the fire-engine and the hosing stuck out on show like some gun.

From great bustle everything was in a muddle; nor did any man in truth know who was to be met; the Governor or the Bishop.

A flight of daws scared by the unaccustomed hubbub settled calmly beneath the blue cupola on the white dome of the church. It was already near midday, but there was still no motor car with the

Governor. Nor was Maria Severyanovna, the wife of the C.P., there, for which reason Alexander Ilitch felt the heat extremely ; indeed, as if burned with fire.

When, thereupon, of a sudden, as so often happens, a constable dashed up with the news : ' Here he comes.'

' Here he comes ! ' ran from the square down the ranks to the bridge.

And in a minute or so those who stood nearer the bridge saw a motor car, speedy in a thick cloud of dust.

The motor seemed it would turn aside towards Nakhabin's sawmill, and appeared to pull up ; pulled up ; and then dashed right away, towards the bridge, over the bridge, towards the square. The triumphal minute had arrived.

Lepetov the Superintendent, who had been in a state of stupefaction since Yeremey the porter had handed him the telegram that informed him alone of the visit of the Governor to Stoudenets, suddenly became silent as if a bucket of water had been thrown over him, and not one tooth fell on another.

Pharaoh the Sexton, with his nose picked to bleeding for sobering purposes, raised one foot on to the plank that united the little bells with the big ; and, like thunder, the church bells clanged out.

Hats off, and all heads were bare.

The Rural Dean raised his cross.

The motor, meanwhile, slowing down, was bumping quietly along, stumbling, as it were, in the potholes.

' Help, Constable, help ! ' The Mayor was crying out in a strange voice, suddenly come out of his stupefaction, and, spreading wide his arms, fell in a squatting heap.

Alexander Ilitch rushed to the door.

The door opened.

And somehow, both legs at once, there sprang from the car

The Pickled Cucumberkin—

and

there at the Examiner's back stuck forward Nakhabin's shovel-beard.

' Hurrah, hurrah ! ' burst from the Boys' Brigade.

And all the bells of Stoudenets were ringing.

*

When the friends of the club were bored by everything—cards and the bar, they usually launched forth on all sorts of contrivances—they drank *with the candle*—in the left hand a candle-stump, in the right a bottle, or they put a bucket of brandy on the carpet and stripped and sat in a ring—baling it out with an iron scoop, the scoop being passed round, as it were easier so.

This evening after the morning's divertisement, which almost cost Oparin the Mayor his life—for a long time the Mayor could not come to himself and squeaked like a bird and recognized no one—after all when everything had ended so well there was no need for the friends to look for amusement to any extravagances; even without them there was enough and to spare of everything.

That evening the culprit of the governorial reception, Lepetov the Examiner, *the Pickled Cucumberkin*, was fêted.

Without the governorial reception Lepetov the Examiner (Nakhabin had brought in the Examiner in his car from Lykov), without all those tiresome and joysome surprises connected with this reception (of all this there will unquestionably be talk till the Rural Dean's next birthday celebration),—society was occupied with family matters.

With the celerity of lightning, as his favourite expression has it, Petrousha Grokhotov did his best to inform everybody of the miracle that had happened to the C.P. and of his hoof ointment. The Vet. proclaimed Antonov's ears to the four winds of heaven. And what was not there said and said over again about the miraculous ears, no trace of which remained !

The story of Noah which fitted the occasion was told to the hearing of all, and Petrousha with all the most infinitesimal detail and with naming of all the beasts in turn,—and for vividness' sake, compared the beasts each to each with the friends present, and made much work with his arms, as it were in the absence of words precise.

' What will happen to Alexander Ilitch now ? ' the ladies asked the Vet.

' Why, they will fall off as clean as if they had never been ! ' Petrousha licked his lips.

' And he won't kick ? '

But what Petrousha let out then—well, it was straight out of Polivanov's Anthology *for adults*, the work of Shvedov the Teacher. And immediately deadly silence came upon all the five club-rooms.

Alexander Ilitch was, as always, a sunbeam, but there was something in him not like himself; a sort of *concentratedness*, as if some exasperating thought would not leave him.

While, in simple language, Alexander Ilitch *wanted to get drunk*.

Maria Severyanovna, coming back from the Devil's Gardens just at the dénouement, when in place of the Governor the Pickled Cucumberkin climbed out of the Nakhabin motor,—well, it is impossible to say that she was exactly pleased. And Alexander Ilitch, in another sense, had got it about his ears.

' Ass ! ' said some one, in that extremely indifferent manner of a man whose next action will be to roll under the table and set up snoring ; ' Ass ! '

And the result was like nothing on earth.

Alexander Ilitch, who had listened obediently for hours to Maria Severyanovna, and heard from her not a few *asses* of all sorts, lost the last grain of patience and swung wide his arm and struck in the face with his fist that one who fell beneath his fist, to wit, the Agricultural Expert, Pratkin the Hog. And then there was a real building of Babel and scattering of tongues, and it almost came to knives, only somebody to shout *fire* was wanting.

Some pulled Pratkin, others Alexander Ilitch, and, as often happens, sides were pummelled, and never the right one. In fact, nobody's side should have been pummelled, simply those two pulled apart. Which, for that matter, did happen in the end. They inquired as to the culprit, they talked over and smoothed down the opponents, and turned again to peaceful life. Alexander Ilitch was obliged, willy-nilly, to drink a glass, and, breaking his oath a second time, he again let himself go.

While Wildboar Vasya (who, drunk, from a corner, had called out *ass* to the C.P.), Wildboar Vasya for some unknown reason considered himself the sole culprit of the whole confusion (although there was no mention of Nyousha Kroutikov),—and Vasya was extracted from under the table. And in the *library*, to the tune of friendly guffaws, they *disembowelled* him, quite senseless, publicly measuring the real *asinine appurtenance*; and, having their game with Wildboar, they swung Lepetov the Examiner, the Pickled Cucumberkin, now legless, after which they sat to supper.

At night Petrousha got carried away, and playing the fool, in his cups, invited himself to show the company tricks.

Petrousha at all costs wanted to swallow a fork, handle first.

' You 've got the wrong end ! ' Rogatkin cried, to instruct him. But Petrousha would not hear a word and stuck the fork into his mouth—and choked.

' Whereas I,' tantalized the Excise Officer from the other end of the table, ' I will stuff a monkey-nut up one nostril and out of the other you 'll see jump a pea-nut ! '

' It 's only by my condescension you 're sitting there beside me,' the Secretary chimed in to his neighbour Rogatkin, ' otherwise you 'd be in jail. Who soaked the dry flour in the river ? '

' You 're pleased to joke, Vassily Petrovitch, 'twas an act of God, a sudden storm.'

Rogatkin shone like a samovar, chuckling into his beard over this *company of gentry*.

But Petrousha had given up the work, and set off telling how they stuck five-inch nails into people's tongues in Petersburg, without any sentence passed either.

Liquor was loosing the friends. Then suddenly through the opened windows came a pig's squeal : ' *Cave !* The Police,' whined out a pleading voice, and a dogcart rattled past the windows.

And to the general delight the voice of Doctor Toroptsov was universally recognized ; Bobrov the E.M. was taking the tipsy doctor to Shtchova for a post-mortem, and that meant no joy-ride and the doctor was crying forth.

And again everything livened up. Conversation passed from tricks to the favourite condemnations of the E.M., and Bobrov was dissected through and through all ways.

But the hour of peaceful sleep was nigh. Yermolai Ignatitch had already set going his *commixtion*, a blend of all kinds of wine with bitter millefoil, millefoil for connoisseurs.

As usual some one tried to undress; and all was well, yet something lacking,—now, whatever could that be ?

The moment moved to emotion had arrived.

Nyemov, Stroisky, Pratkin, and Petrousha struck up their favourite song; Alexander Ilitch, who began with a drawling growl in the bass, fell from stupor to fury : ' Whose business is it if I am drunk ? ' he asserted, hardening his heart, staring straight ahead.

While Saltanovsky—Law worm—thumped on the table with his fist and howled quite apropos of nothing :

> ' *I shall kiss thee to eternity,*'

and Pratkin the Hog wept : ' Why have they insulted me ? ' While some one else from the other end of the room was saying, as if wakening from sleep : ' Well, what about it, live a bit, live a bit—give me some more millefoil ! '

But the cry of ' Help, Constable, help ! ' rang in their ears. Who was this shouting ? Oparin the

Mayor ? Doctor Toroptsov ? No one wanted to know exactly, no one for that matter could have found out. Thought was confused, tongues disobedient, and it was all the same,—Examiner or Governor Lepetov, ass's ears or human Antonovian tears, the E.M. taking the Doctor off or the Doctor the E.M., all the same

Nothing mattered.

Why not ? . . .

For eyes were blocked by tipsy tears :

> *Say not yourself 'twas used your youth to ill,*
> *When I caused all by jealousy for you ;*
> *Say not your curly . . . . has caught a chill,*
> *You wore no knickers all the winter through.*

V

THE LEADER OF LIFE

Half the Summer was showery, half the Summer fine ; and passed quietly.

For that matter, it is not the rule for events to take place in Summer ; it is not the time for it.

In customary manner in the town and round about in the villages there were many fires, both by night and by broad day. Murders are committed on Holy Days, but it is impossible to foresee fires. And frequently they burned all night till dawn, and all night the alarm bell clanged and fire like a pillar moved through the town.

More beer was drunk in the club than in Winter, but on the other hand less vodka and *millefoil* ; your head spins in Summer.

Talk about the Saint's Day *governorial reception* to Lepetov the Examiner, and about the remarkable ears, as was to be reckoned, proved sufficient for the whole Summer. On Trinity Sunday hail larger than the yolk of an egg fell, while on the feast of Saint Peter a *witch* was seen.

Soushkov's kids—Soushkov is a blacksmith, his smithy behind the teahouse, *The Kolpaks*—the little smiths it was brought the first news of the witch ; the kids were running towards the monastery along by the quarry, running home in the evening, and something came up from the quarry to them in white,—a witch.

89

People began to talk, people began to explain. And soon all Stoudenets knew about the witch, and people were afraid for their lives to go past the quarry.

While those daredevils who summoned courage to approach the quarry told of much that was strange, and much that was conflicting ; one that with his own eyes he had seen the barber, Youlin—Grishka Otrepyev—and avowed Grishka was boiling his supper in a cauldron while the witch sat at his side and they were chatting away. While others added to this that the witch had horse's hoofs and human hands ; they too saw it with their own eyes.

Now, Youlin was called Grishka Otrepyev after that fabulous famous squireen of the Troublous Times who sprang lackey to monk, and monk to Job the Patriarch's quill-driver, and quill-driver fled to Poland, and kissed King Sigismund's hand ; and in the dawn of the new century descended again on Moscovy,—Tsar Dmitry Ivanovitch born again, gay pretender.

But why exactly Youlin should get into such other strange company the Devil only knows—Youlin is before everybody's eyes, Youlin alone in all Stoudenets cuts hair and shaves. And it was strange that when the talk got to his ears, at first he was very bold and was ' bashing in the mugs ' of one or two people, but afterwards he grew meek and began to hide himself away somehow suspiciously. Pilgrims coming to the Tikhvin Nunnery in trembling visited the Youlin barber's shop and the unclean quarry, and some from fear swam right across the River Bear, fearing the touch of the unclean. And a regular track would have been made, a *monastery track*, just as in olden times of here the road between Kiev and the *Nightingale Robber*—if Alexander Ilitch himself had not intervened, determined to take the witch by force.

Alexander Ilitch's determination was unshakeable,—in honour firm and unshakeable. And one fine day, drawing a cordon, he surrounded the pit with police while the daredevils descended thither with crowbars and sticks. And then with one weapon and another and some with stones and some with bricks, they began to beat the pit.

And suddenly there sprang out—a dog, ay, and a most terrible one, a shaggy white dog on three legs—followed by pups. They set off on the chase, but her tracks were already cold.

So they let her go.

And however obvious it might be that it was a dog and no witch, and what is more, Yarlykov's bitch Oscar, and that Youlin the Barber had nothing to do with it, all the same they ragged Youlin to the point of his throwing his scissors at them. And one or two of the daredevils found their way into Bobrov's cabinet, and, of course, went straight off to the prison.

And on the day of Saint Elias, as in olden times too, there came running by a track nor foot nor wheel had touched, to the River Bear from the Stoudenets woods, a stag with golden horns ; and the stag dipped its horns in the River Bear. But the water was warm, the Bear River had not grown cold, and the rain of Saint Elias had not sprinkled the earth, and the days had not grown cold. And again the stag on the eve of Ascension Day had perforce to run to the River Bear and again dip in the river its golden horns.

Then on Ascension Day old Mother Spinnilegs surnamed Philipiev gave birth to a devil.

She was nigh the seventies ; and Gennashka, her husband, must be nigh his forties, but otherwise, well, all right, a healthy peasant ; but whether in drink his mouth watered for Spinnilegs' money or she encircled her husband with the twelve keys, somehow, h'm . . . without some special means, h'm. . . . But, Gennashka having no great joy with Spinnilegs, he formed a union with Vassikha the workgirl ; at their teahouse, *The Kolpaks*, she worked.

But can you hide anything from Spinnilegs ? That 's why she *is* Spinnilegs, to know all and about all.

She tried washing herself in honey and then giving it to Gennashka to drink—but this did not help ; so the old woman thought of how to scare him so that to the end of all time he would not want to wander.

Gennashka rode off to Lykov for supplies, Spinnilegs

at home alone. And Spinnilegs heated the bath and called Mrs. Baretkin the Midwife, and there in the bath she was delivered . . . of a little black hairy devil with a little tail! Such was the fruit of her womb.

Mrs. Barètkin goes off to the police : ' Old Mother Spinnilegs has a little black hairy devil with a little tail and its neck twisted,' she reports. They poured some spirit into a jar and stuck Spinnilegs' devil in the jar in the spirit and off to Doctor Toroptsov for examination.

Ivan Nikanoritch, though he is a drinker, has done people not a few kindnesses, and in how many prayers about health does not his name come, and at communion he is mentioned in the liturgy ; and if Ivan Nikanoritch glances at you he can see right through you.

' A still-born kitten ! ' says Ivan Nikanoritch.

' A kitten ? '

Toroptsov is full of faith, but that was a little too much.

' I did not do anything, I have known nothing unclean ; they have fed me with gingerbread ! ' Spinnilegs' voice sang more sonorous than the magic keys ; ' and I conceived and bore from that gingerbread ; Vassikha the workgirl brought the gingerbread from the market and I ate of it and I felt myself heavy.'

But Gennashka was not only scared for all time, —Gennashka went quite off his head ; whom to

release from this life the first, Vassikha the skivvy
or his wife Spinnilegs ? Only this would his mind
contain, he wasted away, grew dark as a devil,
from drink grew thin. And he told every one he
met—all the same story about his devil.

He went himself to Bobrov's cabinet, just like any
little evil one. ' Have you heard, Sergey Alexeyevitch,—excuse my boldness,—my old woman's
given birth to a devil ? '—whispered Gennashka,
looking fearsomely somewhere aside—' that's all
there is left, in a jar at Ivan Nikanoritch's. The
old woman's had a lot of 'em, devils, like litters
of pigs, a whole epidemic of them born ; she let
the first one jump out on to the floor and the Evil
One himself gave him the strength,—that was the
first,—and he scampered off,—but when the second
came up she snatched him and twisted his neck,—
that's the one they got ! '

Gennashka whispered away and in his head span
round :

' whom first release from this life, Vassikha the
skivvy or his wife Spinnilegs ? '

They showed Spinnilegs' devil—kitten—to Bobrov ; Bobrov did not take the matter up.

In the Autumn the assize court came from Lykov
and the sittings began, Bobrov keeping his eye on
all his cases. And all went as it should : the
murderers he had gathered in all condemned, some
to the galleys, others to convict gangs, rarely to
mere imprisonment.

And they gave Soukhov, on trial for arson in Shtchova,—this was a particularly memorable case, both because the fire came on that *hearts and heads of oak* day when the wonderful Antonovian ears and the birthday *governorial reception* given to Lepetov the Examiner, and because they had no little bother making out the case against the man—well, they gave this Soukhov, who confessed to everything in the end, as big a dose as the law allowed.

And there was reason for Bobrov to be satisfied, —it was possible to rejoice—for the law had conquered! And he felt himself particularly in place, firm and in mettle.

But then how terribly it all ended; the culprit turned out not to be the culprit at all; the man was downed for nothing!

About five days after the trial a man, a peasant Balyakin, came to Bobrov from Shtchova and confessed everything; his sin, he, Balyakin, guilty of it all; he set fire to peasant Toropov's house and gave false evidence against Soukhov, and Soukhov had nothing to do with it; Soukhov had stolen a sheep from his old woman, sold it, and drunk it, and had hidden from his old woman—a tartar—in the baths.

' Every guilt guilty,' the little peasant stammered.

Questioning Balyakin, Bobrov despatched him to the police and himself went off to Shtchova to test Balyakin's story on the spot. And in Shtchova, on the spot, everything was now confirmed, and it was not Soukhov set fire to it, but Balyakin, while Soukhov was hiding from his old woman. It was the mistake of the Court Examining Magistrate!

What! He, Bobrov, had made a mistake!

They had twisted him, twisted Bobrov, round their fingers.

The moths will be crumbling our teeth up next!

And this mistake was a stone cast at him, striking him in the heart, immutable and firm, itself a stone and as gall bitter. And he did not feel the bite in his soul, was not afraid because every one who wanted would snatch at that mistake, would trump it far and wide, would tread him underfoot; but that he, Bobrov, had been so cruelly and shamefully deceived.

Yet at first he did not lose his head, no, somehow pulled himself up, as if grown larger.

Yes, he had made a mistake, he was guilty— *every guilt guilty !*—but he would right that mistake; all would be as it should; in his heat the matter seemed simple and clear.

Returning from Shtchova that night Bobrov was turned out of his trap into the deep ditch by Lakoutin's and hurt his side badly against a stone, but was on his feet in a moment as if he had never fallen— he did not notice anything.

How indeed had he time! His work was awaiting him in Stoudenets.

Indeed, his work was particularly necessary to him now. Without it he would have been as helpless as without arms. Without it—no question—he could never breathe again.

Yes, he would put the mistake right—not only that—by work, and by work alone, he would efface that mistake.

God alone knows why things are like that in life ; whether you were born in evil days or under an evil star, you have no peace for the consolation of your soul but a hellish time and misfortune and shame descend on your head till you do not know whose blow will come next, what thing bring you to earth.

*

What was wrong with the life of *Vassilisa the Fair* ? what was amiss in the house of the Chairman of the L.G.B. ? Before, it was bend your back over the pump, frozen through, fingers numbed stiff—whereas now she was in the warm, in the clean, safe as a lamb in the crook of the Good Shepherd's arm—*Madame*, and booted and clothed and fed. It is not so terribly difficult, after all, strolling about a room naked !

But yet, just you wait ! Vassilisa's soul fell sick.

Her soul fell sick, and all grew chill ; the daylight brought no joy, and nigh she was to laying hands on herself.

Vassilisa stirred long in agony, her secret within her—and at night would walk before her *idol*, yet tears stifle her.

97

And it was like a stone—there—she felt it.

While *he* would stretch himself out, lying on the sofa, smoking . . . like a hound would sit there; the doors locked, no one allowed in.

Vassilisa was patient, and still patient, but it was clear now patience was no salvation; *her soul was sick*, and to the old man she decided to go. Vassilisa seized the moment *he* was not at home, and by backyards she made her way to Shapaiev's garden; what the old man said she would do.

Shapaiev received Vassilisa kindly, asked her about it all; and as at confession Vassilisa opened her heart; and the old man diagnosed there was a devil in Vassilisa and the devil could be driven out.

' You must humble yourself,' said the old man, ' you go in velvet, but walk in sin. God forgives all that is natural, but nowhere is it said we should go naked, this is not natural. In front of him you walk about, and the devils, you shameless one, rejoice, by your shamelessness have you inflamed him. You must humble yourself. You do sin by your beauty; now destroy this beauty, abase it! You are grown haughty in your beauty! You must humble yourself! If you go to the church you will deck yourself out—*Vassilisa the Fair !*—but you must cast it underfoot, your beauty, and destroy it !'

And his hands reached out to her.

Vassilisa stumbled back, clouded over—she knew what it would come to, and was afraid.

' Mighty shameful you 've become, eh ? ' croaked the old man, and suddenly, masteringly, all straight, straight at her, ' and I tell you humble yourself, have no mercy on yourself ! '

The old man, why, he is only called that, old man Shapaiev is not really so old ; true, grey and skinny-legged as if frozen in the legs, and that made him tremble all over ; but this thinness, this sinewyness was strong as steel.

And, of course, Shapaiev could manage not only one—a whole legion of devils.

Vassilisa consented to all. And all the money she had she would give him. And Shapaiev began *to drive out the devil.* . . .

Vassilisa the Fair, how will you now go before your Idol ? What will you tell him ? What will he say ? And the club friends ! Why, 'twas for you they wept in that *moment moved to emotion* when they, drunken, sang of *youth used to ill*, Nyemov, Stroisky, Pratkin and Petrousha !

Vassilisa the Fair, still it is not too late, still is there one minute. For verily this is that devil himself, leads you !

And what did she think ? What should she think, with her soul all in pain ! ' My soul is in pain ! ' Let her do all she wants ! But the minute is passed ; it is too late. Shapaiev has been driving out the devil . . . driving out the devil after his own fashion ; Shapaiev howling, lost in howling like the devils. Pugh ! the devil 's not in it !

99

And the devil left Vassilisa.

The old man was all a-tremble—his eyes be-dimmed and his hair limp—suddenly, somehow, stern ; while Vassilisa from joy fell at his feet, kissing his feet, easier she felt ! As if something rolled off her soul, as if all was light and quiet, why, as it used to be before in days when she froze at the pump. She was quite well.

' There, you have humbled yourself, but the sin must still be washed away,' and Shapaiev told Vassilisa to come again. ' There is a prayer of purification ! There is a special prayer ! ' he said sternly, stern, not looking at her.

But not once merely ; three times will Vassilisa come if necessary.

In these times old men quench the fires by sub-mission.

And this is not a time to go in your own paths— man is lost ; man is grown weak, above all, is grown petty ; how can such man from fear for his own skin do great deeds, *save mankind*. For the people have fallen to evil ways.

Verily, and the days are not *beyond the hills* . . . the days are already upon us—on Russia, days of which it is fearful even to tell !

We must make ready, prepare ourselves, temper our souls, strengthen our spirits ; for there are old men

quenching the fires by submission.

And those who are not content with the old men

murmur in revolt; but the old men are inflexible, will hear nothing;

> and they are right.

Let us then look around us, let us then give thought, let us examine ourselves, in all Russia examine ourselves, what are we? what is at the bottom of our souls? much good? what good? and are the weapons of our weak, petty power indeed powerful?

Thus speak the old men.

Those not content with the old men, understanding not their thoughts or their designs, they run betimes, crying:

> ' let us save mankind ! '

> Blind, they undertake tasks and fail; blind, uncertain, they stumble, neither do they love nor desire.

Well, and what will you; chicken strengths, sparrow souls, what will you? what design? what attain? whom help?

Thus speak the old men, and they are right.

Well, it must be admitted every monkey wants to do miracles; with empty hands, cigarette balanced in mouth, they would receive the gift of God.

But temptations increase and life grows more hard.

And of course! for the ape has blundered forward to make miracles, and a blind dribbling scoundrel keeps house.

It was difficult for Vassilisa to get out of the house unnoticed, but yet necessary, to wash away her sin in prayer—the old man had said so. Her soul was lighter, but still it seemed as if something unclean was stuck to her; but as soon as she took the purificatory prayer she would emerge as from the baptismal font. And again Vassilisa awaited her chance, again by the backyards, and to the garden, to the old man.

Why indeed! The Lord had had mercy on her, and she was made whole, if only she could get that prayer; and Vassilisa came to Shapaiev for the prayer.

But evidently that devil when it came out of Vassilisa, hopped straight into the old man, just straight into the old man.

What is that nonsense about a prayer! He could not utter one word, grown green, snuffling like a tomcat at a crack,—and he flung himself at her again and again, wanted . . . and thus he laboured and strained away; his holy image scraping on her breast, his hands — iron; his chest — a smith's bellows.

Vassilisa's whole soul overturned—why, she had committed sin and desired purification by prayer; and there in the unknown, in the secret parts of her heart, everything had burst into flame. 'The accursed one!' Her heart fluttered. She struggled —could not get away.

Vassilisa struggled—no, nothing doing. But no,

he would not let her go . . . yet she got away.
Nothing doing :—and his agile fingers crackled.

She had broken away, and off she ran.

But where to ? Who would hear her ? Who
defend ?

Her idol ? No.

To whom should she go ? Where seek justice ?

Why, of course, to the Examining Magistrate, to
Bobrov ; and off went Vassilisa to Bobrov. Bobrov
heard her out, yet not a word did he speak, and
Vassilisa went away with what she had come. Her
affront he did not remove ; but the matter was put
in legal motion, and of all his cases Bobrov put the
Shapaiev one first : he would show what he was
made of.

Shapaiev could not but know that any one
summoned to Bobrov in the end could not escape
prison. And his peasant women disciples tried to
hide the old man, present their bosom for the blow,
not give him up.

The old man did not care a button.

' I hold converse with the Lord,' he instructed his
women, sheep who understood not, ' I talk to the
Lord every day, and am not afraid ; why should I
fear a detective ? '

And this was true ; Shapaiev spoke without
timidity, without even a grain of timidity. And it
seemed that although Bobrov sat and questioned
and Shapaiev stood before him and answered, it

103

was not Shapaiev come to Bobrov, but Bobrov to Shapaiev, to be examined. The old man did not defend himself. Yes, he had treated Vassilisa by fornication and he had healed her, also he had taken money from her, yes.

'But nothing more.'

Shapaiev even flipped his wiry leg and squinted his eyes suddenly into his nose.

'Who knoweth the Lord, the Spirit of the Lord, his fates are unknown and his ways explored!' And the conversation turned somehow of its own accord in quite a different direction. It was not a case of fornication and devils, nor of money nor outrage. Conversation turned to Bobrov's fortress, to his *Law*, to his unshakeable faith in the Law.

According to Shapaiev there was no crime. There was no crime, but there was misfortune. Misfortune comes from sin; sin stalks through the world, makes division among people. 'Where man is, there is sin too.' The words came like blows of a hammer. And any one involved in sin is not a criminal, but an *unfortunate*. And in all, in this, is God's will—fate; and man should not judge the unfortunate, man should not punish,—in his very misfortune the criminal bears his own punishment—his misfortune.

And indeed if any one is worthy of punishment, then it is not he who had committed the *crime*, but he who has condemned this *criminal*, the punisher of this criminal. 'The sinner, he who is *humbled*, gains much wealth. The sinner, the criminal, is nearer to God, 'tis he who thinks of God, he who prays. The sinner will stand first before God,' the old man said; and great grief and bitter repentance sounded in his voice.

And for a minute Bobrov was prompted to let him return to his home without any consequences, but at once he had himself in hand, and merely moved forward his long, dry fingers.

Shapaiev went on talking.

Shapaiev's speech was full of pertinent phrases; he had an answer for everything and he told fables also.

Whereas the conclusion from all his tangled words and all his fables was something about wise people having hearing, that the people can only be healed by *unselfish deed of effort*, while the *greatest* such deed is that of *voluntary suffering*. ' Turn aside entirely from thyself and leave thyself, take on to thyself the sin of another, take the cross of another and carry this cross for that other.' The words fell like the blows of a hammer. And *voluntary suffering*, this voluntary bondage for another, for the world, would save the Russian nation, enlighten its heart, purify its soul.

Till evening Bobrov retained Shapaiev, not letting him depart.

He essayed to explain his view to him,—that of the Law, but the old man contradicted him. ' You say fine words, but you 've not the least notion of what is fine !' said Shapaiev in fury, and that was the end of the conversation.

Bobrov wrote out his decision—what was there more to be said !—while Shapaiev, his eyes squinting at his nose, stood sullen, muttering something—his prayer.

'Our Most Holy Virgin Mother went through the agonies . . .' Shapaiev said suddenly.

Bobrov laid down his pen for a moment, frowning. Shapaiev got going.

'Our Most Holy Virgin Mother went through the agonies, Michael the Archangel led her, showed her the way . . .' and his voice fell, 'and the Mother of God left paradise. She went of her own accord to suffer, to us, to suffer, to suffer with the unforgiven. And there she suffers and groans for us in her agony, the defendress of the whole world. Between people and the Lord there are threads. . . .'

And he fell silent and stood so grief-burdened and abashed—that it was painful to look at him.

Shapaiev went to prison ; and Bobrov into himself, into that cruel silent life of his.

*

Night come, locked in, Bobrov did not sit up to the table or open a book. His was no mood for reading.

Agitated, tossed from the rut of his usual thoughts, he paced about his room, like a solitary thief, tied in a knot in the examining chamber, back, alone, in his cell. The room oppressed him; but where could he find more space? The mistake about the fire would not leave his head; and Shapaiev's words stood, a memory for all time.

For perhaps he had made mistakes before this too, not only once, but, well, they were never noticed? Did he really know what was fitting? And he had the feeling of a search. And it would not quit him, only it was not the incendiary he pursued, but himself.

Whereupon, for the first time for many years, he asked himself—if he was right in his *Law*? and was the Law the salvation of Russia?

When his coachman Fartounin had pitched him out he had felt something turn over inside him, but forgot about it then as if he had not noticed it. But at this moment he remembered it, remembered it because something *in his soul* turned over; and a piercing pain approached his heart.

What would save Russia, if not his Law? Unselfish deed of effort, voluntary suffering? But his Law; what should happen to the Law? And he, the Examining Magistrate, did Russia need him? When should *he* go?

Something had turned over in his soul, in the unknown depths of his heart, and he could no longer return to past nights with their fury and their curse, would not think as of old, direct his thoughts along those beaten tracks. And those painful places he had so many years avoided—preserving himself for his sacred book, for the denunciation become, like brandy, habit—were laid bare, and with that choking ache of the soul with which he remembered it only during those first years of their division, he remembered that night when he was called to his wife. '*I know, I know everything!*' her voice rang clearly over him,—those words of hers, —he felt the injury of it all. And sorrow for it all —for his life thus pointlessly wasted.

But how pointlessly? Why, but he had given his life in defence of the Law, in the defence of the Russian people nigh to destruction from lawlessness. He had been doing the work of his faith. He had served in everything for Russian justice, seeking justice and a defence for the people. He was all for Russia.

But, of course, this had to be settled somehow.

His heart was eaten into, his fortress undermined ; but he would not give in.

He ; did he then know what was right ?

And if all his Law went to the devil, why was Shapaiev's *voluntary suffering* right ? To take guilt on oneself ; what, and that scoundrel move free about his villany, and laugh too ! And that was right ? For whom ? For Russia ? And of course, turn him the other cheek !

But then he will not strike me alone,—just let him, just try,—hold thy peace ! And, of course, love them that hate us ! People forgive any villain, that 's why there is so much villany. And Russia is crushed by this inrooted *holding of her peace*, grown stupid, grown beastlike from this submissiveness. And this is right ? For whom ?

The air grew thick ; vodka drew him. I go murdering, and some one else will take my guilt on himself ! Whereas I shall murder because sin has *entangled* me, and there is nothing against sin—God's will in all !

God's will !

And, murdering, I, an unfortunate, shall bear my own punishment in this my misfortune. While the judge who by the Law condemns me—since of course they will try me, for of course everybody will start off 'mid original sin, in the Kingdom of Fate and Sin, everybody to the last man is not to be expected to begin *living the holy life* !—and the judge, Nalimov, will then bear his punishment for his most legal condemnation ?

For whom ? For whose account ? For Russia ?

The vodka was burning him, and he was in pain ; the vodka burned him.

' And if you let people do everything they want,' Bobrov suddenly asked himself, ' let them go, let everything be possible,—even if only for one single day possible ? ' And he answered ' People are at bottom coarse, stupid beings and savage ; and in one day, in one single day, perhaps, they might not do anything, the temptation would be so great they would not know what to start with, would lose their heads. . . . And I ? What would I do in that one single day ? '

Bobrov frowned, and sat thus a long time.

' I know, I know everything ! ' he whispered.

And again that last night passed through his memory.

The hour of the dispersal of the club was drawing near. There the hearts of the club drunk from wine grew faint for Vassilisa the Fair burning to them like a distant star.

The shutters thundered from outside—the club friends were returning to their beds past Bobrov's house ; and something pierced his heart at that blow ; his heart stopped. ' There it is, the end,' flashed through his mind.

And at once so much was forgotten,—how strange,—and even the sacred book with the denunciation and curse of the Russian people by which all his strength and fortress was held,—forgotten as if it had never existed.   And a repose of helplessness ensued : the will of the Lord in all !

Then his heart again beat as it always beat, but he did not venture to stir. Terrible, terrible, and pain lest *that* seize him again.

In the corner hung an icon, the same one that his father had, before which once upon a time his father used to pray :—the Virgin . . . *My Soul doth Magnify the Lord.*

' There are threads between people and the

Lord,' Bobrov remembered Shapaiev's words, and his head was crushed into his shoulders as his father's used to be when the old man prayed. . . .

And suddenly he felt ashamed. Quickly he poured out another glass, and, as if set on fire, sprang to his feet : ' What the devil does this people want with your Law ! Neither you to it, nor it to you, is necessary. The indefensible, rebellious . . . the accursed people ! ' And as by custom he raised his fist, his rod—the Law—the death-dealing sign, the cross raised on high, his rod, cross, and curse—and alone he would go with this severed from the whole people, alone, to the end of the world, into *the desert where no man lives*—a stone recoiling. While in his soul all was churned up—in the unknown secret deeps of his heart. And his soul was like a rag rent asunder. The earth trembled under him and agonizingly the vodka burned. Yes, all in him burned ; his mind burned, his heart burned, his soul burned.

It was Soukhov, the incendiary Soukhov ;—*he* lit this fire.

Bobrov made a final effort, swallowed again—at one gulp ; and things, it seemed, began to clear.

Carefully he went to the couch, put out the light.

When in Petersburg still as a student Bobrov had fallen ill of that illness considered petty about which it is customary to talk no more seriously than of some trifling cold in the head . . . and used to go home from the doctor in the evening along the Nevsky . . . he somehow felt himself near to everybody; he met so many people damaged, people in sin, like himself—all brothers and sisters. . . . And how fine it would be suddenly to appear in the club to-morrow and pass the evening there, like every one else, with them all. And all would be made peaceful in good humour, as it should, and life would start again well and cool and merry, sorrowless, without this heart-sore.

Or should he pay Florry a visit?

And thus, the happiness of the club pouring like holy oil on to his soul, *the anointment of fornication*, with thoughts of Florry the Whore he rolled over, and bitter sleep embraced him.

He dreamed a confused, bitter dream.

It happened there was a new servant in the house, a healthy wench, like Vassilisa; and it seemed she came into his room holding huge scissors in her hand, and kept snipping at the air and playing about with the scissors like Youlin the Barber—Gregory Otrepyev—getting ready to cut. Nearer and nearer the wench came to him, and the nearer she came the more restless he was, and dark fear fell upon him, and he screwed himself up, crouched together, squeezed in—hand to hand, leg to leg—

—'absolve thou me!' : 'I absolve thee not!'

—'save thou me!' : 'Evil one, I save thee not!'

—'have mercy on me!' : 'There is no mercy!'

No mercy, no mercy for him, and he tossed about, turning his head, this way and that, but there was no escape.

112

VI

HARVEST OF TOIL

In the morning at the customary hour Bobrov rose —depressed and weak, broken by his dream.

Ice-cold water did not help.

He was all crumpled, shrunken, limp; his whole body ached as if he had been belaboured with cudgels; and everything was burdensome to him.

'But if he went away to Paris! He should go away to Paris!' he seized at the last straw,—and live there, and no one know who he was. There he would quietly live out his last days. There the air was so light! In the evening he would hear the sound of bells, the hour at the Sorbonne, the Sénat, the Saint-Sulpice striking. . . . He bent his ear to listen, as if he would then in all reality hear it— from the town of happiness, the capital of the world, the good news would come to him. And for a minute Paris stood before him clear to the point of pain; a clouded, grey evening of May. . . .

But there was his trained canary singing the anthem . . . God save the Tsar. . . .

Bobrov got up It was difficult to dress. He felt his uniform frock-coat crush him, his woollen vest rough to the skin, scratching chest and back, as it were a barbed torture-jacket, needle-studded chains, had been clad on him.

With great effort Bobrov went down, went to his cabinet. Parmyon Nikititch the secretary, in his figured pale blue shirt, was already at the table and his short trousers were turned up higher than ever; everywhere outside was impassable mud, and though the surface was drying a little precaution was never amiss.

The day began as it always did with correspondence and documents. Then witnesses began to come.

A father had quarrelled with his son—peace was being made between them. 'Bow you down to his feet, you scoundrel; your head won't fall off! And you, you forgive him!' Parmyon Nikititch was instructing.

But somehow it was all the same to Bobrov.

And whatever Kariev might say, even if he banged their heads together, he did not care. It had no point.

A policeman brought in a man under arrest. He had to be examined quickly. This Bobrov was accustomed to do; this was easy, and he soon dealt with the arrested man.

The interval arrived. Parmyon Nikititch left the room. Bobrov, however, remained—alone at his table. His tea grew cold, but he did not stir, sat where he had taken his seat. Thoughts went heavily, darkly and heavily, and anyhow, to no point, whatever came into his head.

And for some reason or other he remembered a case, such a trifling one, he had read it in the paper. Somewhere, in Vladivostock, a Chinaman was being tried.

114

The Chinaman knew Russian very badly, and understood even less. They tried him without an interpreter. They were trying him for stealing a pair of trousers.

' Did you steal a pair of trousers ? ' the magistrate asked. ' One piecie trousah,' the Chinaman answered in a firm voice.

' Did you steal one piecie trouser ? '

' Stole one piecie trousah.'

Well, and the magistrate reads out the sentence : ' For the theft of one pair of trousers so-and-so is sentenced to so many strokes of the cat.'

What was that, for a pair of trousers ? The Chinaman is amazed, cannot understand, will not submit.

' *One* piecie trousah ! ' the Chinaman cries out, the words tearing from his soul in a despairing cry ; but the sentence is already in force, and they lead him away.

' One piecie trousah ! ' Bobrov gulped air ; something stabbing at his heart. And he grew tranquil. A daw was sitting on the window-sill—its eyes were white. Bobrov stared at that daw as if petrified. He could not tear himself from its white eyes. It sat, would not fly away. It stared at Bobrov with its white eyes. A shiver ran over his body. ' I must shut the window,' Bobrov thought. And he did not stir, only screwed up his eyes. And in his eyes danced two white specks. And something was stabbing at his heart.

' No interpreter, we all are without an interpreter.
. . . The judge condemns us and we are bewildered ;
we cry out, but it is too late. . . .'

Bobrov snatched at the Chinaman, thinking, no
doubt, that with the Chinaman he could drive out
the daw ; but even with closed eyes he still saw it
alone, the daw sitting quietly on the window-sill,
staring straight at him with the white eyes.

' Yes, without interpreter . . . and with what
indignation, cruelly, unjustly sentenced, do we go
to our prison ! A pair of trousers ? . . . *One piecie
trousah !* ' and Bobrov started up from the pain.

Parmyon Nikititch was on tip-toe closing the
window. His trousers were still shortened, his
wide, well-worn rubbers were gaping and his grey
cotton socks were visible. And work began again.

Bobrov somehow made a final effort to restrain
himself ; it was painful to look at him ; and again
he was signing papers, his hand guiding itself, and
again he was examining, questions forming themselves from long habit. The stink of fusty sheep-
skins overpowered him. Wearily, slowly, the hours
passed.

At last there were no others. There was no one
to wait for. Parmyon Nikititch opened the case-
ments, tied up his goloshes, and it was possible to
go one's way, as usual, in silence. At this moment
a corporal came in with a packet ; ' The Ouripino
L.G.B. Officer, Kroupkin, has shot his wife.'

Bobrov thrust the packet into his pocket ; but

116

instead of sending for the horses, he went slowly upstairs.

*

In Alexander Ilitch's room under the famous cross-wove carpet of the hair of twelve divers wolves, Alexander Ilitch himself was sitting after dinner at the gramophone, and with him Rogatkin the L.G.B. man.

' My nose itches ! ' winked Alexander Ilitch.

' You should have some vodka.'

' With pleasure.'

' Well, put on something a bit merrier ! '

Rogatkin, smirking into his beard, shone like a samovar ; and the gramophone scrooped away with all its might ; and Alexander Ilitch and Semyon Mikheitch were both very satisfied.

Rogatkin's business, about which he had come to talk with the Police Captain (some official catering) had been settled to mutual advantage ;—Rogatkin not out of pocket, and Maria Severyanovna not exactly losing ; no loss (on the contrary, gain) to the *Devil's Gardens*. Live and . . . be merry !

It had long been time to go to the club ; there would follow some *keeping out the cold*—'twas no sin to let oneself go, *pegging down* such an occasion. And Alexander Ilitch sneezed away like a dog from satisfaction.

The friends happened to drop in at the same moment. All were there. The elder Ivan Feoktistovitch Bogoyavlensky, Nalimov, Stepan Stepan-

itch, the Judge ; the L.G.B. Officer Nikolai Vassilye-
vitch Saltanovsky—*Law worm* ; the Excise Officer
Shverin, Sergey Sergeitch, *Table d'hôte* ; the
Agricultural Expert Pratkin, Semyon Fyodorovitch
the Hog ; and the Secretary of the Town Council
Vassily Petrovitch Nyemov ; and the Tax-Collector
Vladimir Nikolaievitch Stroisky, *Don Juan* ; and
the Postmaster Arkady Pavlovitch Yarlykov ; and
the Forester Kourganovsky, Erast Evgrafovitch
the Water-trough ; and Anna Savinovna Shverin, and
Katerina Vladimirovna Toroptsov, *Country Kate* ;
and Prascovia Ivanovna Bobrov, the E.M.'s wife ;
and Ivan Nikanoritch Toroptsov himself, who had
succeeded in sitting out if not the whole nineteen,
at least a dozen of them.

The latest news occupied everybody ; the Local
Government Board Officer Kroupkin shooting his
wife like a hare ; and this piece of news outshadowed
the Byelozerov scandal with Vassilisa the Fair.

Kroupkin had always been a welcome guest when
he came to Stoudenets. He was no longer young,
but strong, with a military bearing, and with his
bird's eye had enticed away Saltanovsky Law-worm's
wife ; but the chief thing was that he was famed
for his shooting, a great sportsman, kept nine
borzois, and always took advantage of the first snow
to wreak destruction on hares. And everybody
was so afraid of him they did not dare kill hares.

But this is what happened ; the son of the Chairman of the Parish Council in Ouripino, a soldier,

came home and brought a gun with him and began mercilessly shooting hares. Kroupkin heard of it and fined the soldier; twenty-five roubles fine and a few days as well. The soldier appealed to the district authorities and they lessened the sentence according to law. The soldier paid the fine and went back to the hares. Others followed his example.

Kroupkin went mad, dealt fines right and left. And they all appealed to the district authorities. Then the provincial authorities interfered, paper after paper, and it almost came to a reprimand on a complaint from the district authorities.

'Kroupkin got furious,' related Petrousha, 'fining two quarts of brandy per hare, and these hares by this time hopping him sick, belly to gullet. He could not sleep at night, there they were in all the corners crawling about, sitting in heaps, white, grey, all colours. And he had a hallucination in the night that a hare jumped on to his bed, he snatched at his gun, aimed, hit . . . struck a match, blood on the bed—the whole charge into his wife.'

The ladies oh-ed and ah-ed.

But Petrousha did not pull up there, and, addressing himself more to the ladies, and particularly to the E.M.'s wife, began telling of some application of *hare's hair* he avowed could cause disaster faster than any hare. The atmosphere was getting thick.

Conversation flagged—that stupid moment—'twas time to talk about Bobrov.

Of course, the E.M.'s mistake about the arson case was held up to ridicule. Like pure holy oil—*anointment from heaven*—the cherished thought that this was at last the end of the Examining Magistrate poured in on every one's soul. 'God grant they take him away from Stoudenets!' Indeed, as what an evil-doer—a wild beast, a wolf, a destroyer, did not Bobrov uprise in their heated phantasy!

'Heh, but our fine beauty's gone one too far!'

'Put his foot in it!'

'Up the pole!'

'They 'll curry him; they 'll razzle him!'

'So they should!'

'Serve him right!' chimed the friends' voices in a round.

Somebody proposed drinking to Bobrov's mistake. Millefoil appeared and houra they shouted. And everything was well, yet something lacking;

now, what could that be?

*

At *The Kolpaks*, Mother Spinnilegs' teahouse, in the cramped living half, the hostess, Mother Spinnilegs herself, Gennashka, and one of the Tikhvin Nuns, Asenepha, were sitting at the samovar.

Gennashka was drinking enchanted water of twelve keys, *with a bite* of the Virgin's bread in place of sugar to take the taste away. Every day Gennashka drank eight cups. Mother Spinnilegs herself prepared the water for him; twelve keys of chests of drawers, cupboards and chests, washed clean with soap, were put in water and the water was heated with them until it boiled, when it was ready and had a disgusting rusty taste. Gennashka drank this water and was in just as bad a state as ever.

And Asenepha was drinking tea *with despite* and the second samovar was already being brought in for the visitor. Asenepha was telling them about the miraculous holy lamp which did miracles and brought healing. The chief holy object in the Nunnery was the miraculous image of the Mother of God of Tikhvin. People offer candles to the icon round which burn a multitude of lampadkas.

And among them is one inextinguishable Imperial Lampadka.

Now, the *furbisher* to Babakhin, the Marshal of Nobility, drove to the Nunnery on a *pilgrimage*, and in his earnestness placed a threepenny candle before this image, and Mother Asenepha stands at this image and patrols it, and she thereupon decided that as soon as she had lit the oil she would leave the *furbisher's* candle to burn through the night and put out the inextinguishable lampadka.

'I put the lampadka out, my dear,' related Asenepha, 'I locked up the church and went into the warmed chapel to vespers. There, my dear, I stand at vespers, and begin thinking what have I done—now, I think, there is the imperial lampadka, inextinguishable, and out of meanness I go and put it out and I thought about it so much I could not pray; the prayer would not come. That's a bad thing, I thought, now I've done, and off I hurried to the church. I opened the door, and look, and there was that little lampadka burning away. The Queen of Heaven herself gave it light—the seven-tongued flame; then sin again came on me, and—let me see, thought I—and put it out again. I put the lampadka out and shut up the church and went into my cell, and when I came in in the morning, there was that little lampadka burning away. . . .'

And Spinnilegs, nodding to the nun's words, overjoyed now she had scared Gennashka for all eternity and separated the peasant from the skivvy, a-hah, began trumpeting her trump too:

'You know, my dear, for me to give birth would be like' . . . and compared it to such an act that Mother Asenepha only gave a decent cough.

Meanwhile Gennashka was drinking his key water and thinking and thinking—whom first to release from this world, Vassikha the skivvy or his wife Spinnilegs; and should he not do miraculous Mother Asenepha at the same time when he was about it?

*

Opposite the white stone prison, opposite the barred windows, against the wall stood three women, they *who come uncalled*.

The day had been chilly and the night was setting in cold and starry with a wind. In an upper window behind the iron bars a yellow prison lamp shone dully. There behind the bars sat three men; Soukhov condemned for the fire, Balyakin the man who lit it, and old Shapaiev—and it was difficult to tell who was the old man, who the incendiary, who the condemned.

The women stood wearily.

The wind howled; the stars twinkled in the night —the lamps of God, the Autumn stars, cold as night itself.

Who would save them by prayer, who bring them out on the way of salvation, who release them, who snatch from the final terrible response—torture eternal and frightful?

By the seven mortal sins had they sinned;

> they had sinned from beginning to end,
> from earth to heaven,
> from earth to the pit,
> from south to north,
> from west to east.

And their sins were more than the stars of night and the leaves of Spring, more than the blades of grass and the sands of the seashore, or the stones, the trees, the beasts, the animals, the birds or the fishes; more than the waves in the sea or drops of rain in the storm, or man and all beings from the beginning of time to the end;

> they had not fed the hungry,
> they had not given drink to the thirsty,

they had not taken the traveller by the wayside
into their home,
they had not clothed the naked,
they had not visited the sick,
they had not come to those sitting in dungeons.

And ceaselessly did they pray into the long night
beneath the cold stars. And they saw as it were
an old man, loving and beloved, knowing the secrets
of their hearts. Unattainably in the self-illumined
light of the supreme third starless heaven, *the
heaven of heavens*, stood the grieving old man in the
air. ' Oh, Lord, defend and have mercy on us !
Lord, have mercy ! Lord, warm our hearts ! Lord,
hearest not Thou me ? '

There behind the white stone prison on the old
graveyard the wind howled.

The wind blew and howled, whirling round the
rotting crosses ; and the crosses, like the heavy
ripened ear in the field, bent low—and one alone
stood firm as it had been placed, the heavy monument to the merchant of Stoudenets, Maxim Ivanov,
did not turn its head :

beneath this stone
lies maxim ivanov merchant
should have lived in enjoyment
but he were pleased to
depart this life

*

Nyousha Kroutikov was drowsing over her

machine, and it was sweet to doze to that clicking.
And suddenly Nyousha sprang up as if Wildboar
Vasya had pricked her. The ribbon was clicking
out as usual ; but the words were unusual ; a cipher
telegram from Lykov to Antonov, Police Captain.
. . . Nyousha flew like a swallow to hand the news
on, but her neighbour was not there.

Wildboar Vasya had gone out *to take the air*—a
starry night—Wildboar stood still, admiring himself,
admiring his magnificent *appurtenance*.

*

> *O little pillow, little pillow*
> *Little pillow billowy* . . .

the Bobrov
girls were singing quietly ; Pasha, Katya, and Zina,
their *Carol*

> ' *Little pillow billowy.*'

They sing it at girls' parties on the eve of marriage,
and in the evenings when the young man comes to
his love.

The girls sang quietly and their voices faded,
drawling

> *Him whom I love, him whom I love, I kiss*
> *him fair,*
> *My pillow, pillow billowy I share* . . .

In his heavy uniform frock-coat and his stone
collar and his prickly, burning, barbed torture-jacket
Bobrov was lying on the couch. As soon as he had

reached his room he had stretched out on the couch and lay there.

A candle was burning on the table. It was flickering—the draught from the window.

Bobrov lay without opening his eyes.

He was feverish with a chill. He wanted to get up, wrap himself up warmly and have a drink ; if only one gulp.

But he lay there and could not call any one.

His thoughts went at random, his heart thumped or died down at random. His will was gone to rags. And in this state he did not want to call anybody.

The curtains of his memory rose. Such distant, chance forgotten things passed before him, but such beloved things, and with the pain of irreparable loss.

Something recalled a certain police report to him ; he had composed it shortly before his marriage, when he was articled clerk in Lykov ; in the luggage department of Lykov Station a basket had been found and in the basket a murdered woman. The words, word for word, stood out in fire :

> The victim is a rather stout woman, of about thirty years of age. She is lying with her head turned aside. She is wearing a black blouse of fashionable cut, a skirt and a petticoat. On her feet are fashionable laced boots. When the left arm of the victim was raised huge maggots crawled across the basket. . . .

And it suddenly became clear to him that the murdered woman in the basket was—his wife, Prascovia Ivanovna.

' How simple,' he thought, ' of the earth earthy, as I am, as all are. . . .'

But memory was already raising another curtain, giving him no time to breathe or think or realize what was happening. Somebody above his will more powerful, stronger, without asking him whether he wanted it or not was having his way with him.

How long ago this was. He was sitting in a tramcar, going to the Smolny, opposite him a woman in a black plush blouse ; her face like a carrot, her nose like a carrot, red, all swollen from tears, in her hands an icon, the Virgin.

Yes, yes, the Virgin—*My Soul doth Magnify the Lord.* Firmly with both hands he was holding her, pressing her to his breast, she rocking to and fro like some one drunk, her eyes lowered to the ground to her shoes in holes ; and suddenly she cried out : ' Take me, take me where you will ! '

' Take me where you will ! ' cries in him too the final voice of final despair.

'Where do you want to go ? Where are you going?'

' To Petersburg Street.

' So that 's it, Petersburg Street.'

' But that 's not the way, that 's not at all the way.'

Him whom I love, him whom I love, I kiss him fair,
My pillow, pillow billowy I share . . .

wail the voices; the Bobrov girls through the wall
are singing—their voices droning on.

'Take me where you will!' the woman shrieks
aloud. And there, raising eyes from pain, worn by
suffering like his mother, rocking as a person drunk
—*Vassilisa the Fair*.

And suddenly it became clear to Bobrov that it
was not his mother, not Vassilisa the Fair, no, not
at all, he himself was groaning. . . . And his final
will collects its final energies in order for all to be
quite inaudible, quite quiet. . . .

'Papa, are you ill?'

Katya, his third daughter, by the Government
Attorney, had come into the room.

'It's all right,' Bobrov raised his eyes, 'Katya.
I . . . it's all right!' and turned face to the wall.

And everything seemed verily to turn over within
him.

He was in the judge's cabinet.

He, Bobrov, was standing before the judge;
Nalimov the Judge was trying him.

But he understood very little of what the judge
was saying to him; although Nalimov was talking
his own mother tongue, it was in some manner of
his own, hard to make out. And only one thing
was clear to him, that he, Examining Magistrate of
the Court, State Councillor by rank, was being
tried. Yes, he was guilty, he had made a mistake.
And there they have condemned him. What?
For one mistake and so severely?

And he wanted to say something in his own justification, wanted to justify himself, but it was too late, the judge was taking off his chain. Then some Chinamen seized him by the sleeves. . . . 'One piecie trousah!'

Bobrov tossed, gulped the air; his heart chilled, his heart stopped; and it became silent in the room, silenter than ever before. The flame flickered—the wind whirled outside the window.

The girls were not singing—all had grown peaceful in their maiden thoughts through the wall; the voices were not dragging their maiden song.

Wide and thundering our highway villainous wind, the songs of the wind, dragged . . . the heart dragged . . . the sea dragged . . . the sea there— is it the sea in turmoil?

There, burning heats,—the earth parching, the heavens raining not, the grasses fading; there the agony,—the unmeasurable weeping? groans and the cry never-ceasing?

There passion unslakeable, storm, destruction unending, the wail unconsoled.

The songs of the wind dragged, the highway villainous wind—the thundering wind whirling afar. . . . .

'Papa!' cried Katya.
But no one answered her.
Only the flame leapt.
And the silence ominously dragged.

Inaudibly Katya went up to the couch, not breathng, bent down.

'Papotchka! My own papa! Papotchka!' and taggered back.

With stony opened eyes, in his heavy uniform rock-coat pitifully there lay Bobrov, and vapour rose rom his mouth.

THE HISTORY OF
THE TINKLING CYMBAL & SOUNDING BRASS
IVAN SEMYONOVITCH STRATILATOV

The English version is dedicated

to

PRINCE D. SVYATOPOLK-MIRSKY

Among the noteworthy objects of our town, after the ancient Prokopiev Monastery with the miraculous image of Theodore Stratilat, the high wooden newly-painted walls of the other one (that is to say, of the Nunnery of the Conception), and the dusty boulevard waggishly illuminated by a single paraffin-lamp hung, and here too was a touch of waggishness, on a rope between the restaurant and the band-stand ; after Berkhatov's Inn, famous for its fennel gherkins done just right in some sort of extraordinary pickle and for its succulent white cabbage—the Seafoam ; after the idiot girl Sister Matrena, whom some worshipped, some told their troubles to, and still others swore at ; finally, after the Sussanin Monument, you would be shown Ivan Stratilatov.

And all who knew the least bit about such matters were in full agreement and unanimity. People would sooner quarrel about the monastery or the nunnery, the antiquity of which had actually been proved by the local learned commission of antiquities itself ; sooner would some cabboony from across the Volga doubt in the boulevard or in the said cele-brated monument ; but in Stratilatov,—nobody, never ! That was an impossibility.

In his twentieth year he had commenced his service in the court in the long, narrow, smoke-blackened office of the criminal department, on the second floor, and fully forty years had flown by this time, many secretaries been changed, and still more articled clerks—all an invading world of strangers,—while he sat eternally there on his own, behind a large table, jagged by knife-cuts, at the window which gave on to the wall of the hotel against which firewood has been piled from time immemorial, and copied out documents.

Just talk to him a bit; whom doesn't he know, what governors whom everybody has now forgotten doesn't he remember? Why, as for governors—he remembers the first president of the first court!

That's Adrian Nikolaievitch sitting there. True, he has a rich head of hair—a bishop's comb wouldn't go through it,—but all the same he's found time to drink his legs off; and however much Lykov the secretary may play the wise man, dumping the legless paralysed clerk in the archives cupboard under lock and key to teach him better, he will drink his seventh head off, too. No, Stratilatov is no fellow of Adrian Nikolaievitch's, and their tables do not stand in a row, but one opposite the other, and it is not for nothing the typewriter has been stood between them: Ivan Semyonovitch has not known what vodka is from the day he was born; and what is more, the articled clerk's gasper in its thin little mouthpiece never seduced him; he did not smoke.

'But that's why I'm alive and well,' Stratilatov would explain, 'I've got through sixty years and

I 'll live to a hundred, I 'll live to a hundred, I 'll start a second hundred : in the early days of this world the righteous lived to five hundred and all that ! '

According to Loukyan the caretaker, everything had gone smoothly with Ivan Semyonovitch for forty years, and there had been no change ; he was always whole as a red berry or an egg. Let us admit that this was not quite accurate—Loukyan was blind in one eye, could not see out of the left ;— but all the same Ivan Semyonovitch was still a fine fellow and strong as a horse-radish, whatever you may say. Of course, of that curly black hair about which Stratilatov's tongue more than once ran away with itself, of those curls—shh ! a curtain on their effect, the pining maids from hopeless love declining —well, 'twas all so smooth and clean, but a bald pate, eyebrows to nape remaining, a wonderful expanse ! But what did that matter, it was even more convenient to be bald ; it meant less expenditure on olive oil ; and it is easier to kill a fly on a bald pate ; and, what 's more, it suited him somehow. There 's the under government-attorney obliged to have his hair cut hedgehog-fashion, and his hands big and white like white gloves with a little ruby on his little finger ; while Ivan Semyonovitch's hands were of the most ordinary, with fingers like little shovels.

' Baldness is an ornament to a man,' said Ivan Semyonovitch himself, not without pride.

The other caretaker, into whose hand Ivan Semyonovitch considers it his duty to slip some salutary little picture every Saturday, is just like Loukyan, decrepit; and although both eyes work he too can see no change, and only points out the ears, as somehow or other Ivan Semyonovitch's ears stick a long way to the side and are lengthy beyond all reason; and indeed it did seem that in those days when Stratilatov's deceased mother was still alive and Stratilatov was famed as the first huntsman in the town,—indeed it did seem they did not stick out quite so much from under the black curls, had not such a tendency to go up to a point.

But the truth must be spoken; the ears were big—enormous—there is no disputing it. But just take a look when Ivan Semyonovitch is sleeping; slip unobserved into his bedroom when, after lunch, sprawled out on the unshaken mattress with his head thrown back on to the pillow greasy as a pancake, he lies on his shaky-legged iron bedstead— they are not at all bad, they nestle like leaves into the pillow, and you wouldn't notice them at once. The cause of it all without doubt is that little grey jockey-cap with a button which Ivan Semyonovitch wears—that causes it.

There remain only his spectacles. Stratilatov will not venture one step without them; they are always on his nose—and they are not clear ones, like Adrian Nikolaievitch's, but smoky, eye-protectors ; while under the glasses, half hidden by their lids, are dull little eyes with whites all yellowish, you know, with little red veins.

That 's how it really is ; though for that matter Ivan Semyonovitch himself makes quite a different assertion,—that spectacles are just the same as goloshes,—he wears them more for the look of the thing, but his eyes are blue. But one never knows what tricks the devil may play, and maybe his eyes really are blue and it is only under the smoky glasses they seem so dull with yellowish whites—an optical delusion, that is to say.

Sixty years Stratilatov has heard ring out, the seventh decade has begun, and it is forty years that he sits there in the court and copies out documents ; and during all those forty years not once has he missed a day, and during all those days not once slacked at his work, and as for change—but what change ? At the baths under the steam if he only pulls in his belly a bit he could very well pass for his assistant Zabalouiev (and the clerk Zabalouiev is the devil of a lad).

' This dog's old age ! ' Adrian Nikolaievitch would say with a smirk, winking under his spectacles at his colleague.

And the legless fellow talked like that, of course, more to be scornful, to jeer, or simply from envy, since he always was and will be, according to Ivan Semyonovitch's well-aimed definition, beset with a devil.

And, in fact, what other point could there be in this ' dog's old age,' taking turn with

> ' Hecuba,' ' Golgotha,'
> ' demurrage,' ' specimen,'
> ' globe,' ' rout,'

and similar expressions like nothing on earth, or at least having no connection whatsoever with Stratilatov ; there the legless one sits copying documents, or composing an application, or smoothing his lumpy ginger beard with the five fingers of his hand ; and then, suddenly, half-seas over, lets something of that sort across the table, and thereupon all the clerks simply flood into laughter, just as if they would die of it.

Well, if you believe any twaddle, talking with a legless person you 'll make a fool of yourself, and it 's putting it pretty mild to say ' beset with a devil.'

But the deacon of All Saints, Prokopy, in whose house Stratilatov has made his nest, is another matter. Prokopy, when conversation turned on the unprecedented vigour and exterior, flourishing out of all accordance with years, of his indefatigable tenant, referred to Nature.

' Nature,' the deacon would say, tugging at his thin red beard, ' it is nature ; her fundamental laws cannot be set at nought.'

And, if you will, the deacon was right.

Round and firm as an egg, with a rosy hue in his cheek, and what a rosiness—real raspberry colour—

and lips the hue of lilac,—you won't match it with any other ; and on his upper lip down just as if it had been blacked with charcoal and stayed so since last carnival, and a nose—you could espy it three miles away—long, and a full, pellucid sort of one, a sugary one.

' When I get old I will grow a beard,' Ivan Semyonovitch, shaved to blueness and here and there scratched a bit from too fastidious application of the razor, would announce, not without satisfaction, and stretch himself up vainly on his thin wiry little legs,—ay, and all that belly a-tremble.

Sturdily thus would he rise, his bald pate open to the sun, vigorously and firmly borne up, on his huge, heavy feet as if to proclaim, There, There I Am, a Head.

And all were agreed as one man that Stratilatov was A Head such as there are few of, but that same Adrian Nikolaievitch here too did not let slip the chance of showing his teeth.

' That 's not a Head you 've got,' the legless one would smirk, ' that, my good fellow, is a Door-Knob ! '

Every day, in the morning, at about seven o'clock, when sleep is still wandering about the houses,— the last sleep, but for that very reason sweet and so deep that neither the falling of logs nor the chime of bells—and they ring every morning in the Prokopiev Monastery and the Nunnery of the Conception and in the parish churches—nothing on earth, it seems, can overcome it and drive it through the door into the hall, when only the market-women with milk and baskets are about on their way to the market and shouting as only market-women can, and clerks are running to the government buildings, in this early bustling hour,—if you go down Cat's Alley ten to one you will come face to face with Stratilatov.

In winter he is in a padded overcoat, a red worsted scarf wound about his neck, in summer in a grey lustring jacket and a grey jockey cap with a button, and a speckled handkerchief inevitably sticking out of his pocket, and under his arm a blue paper bag of sugar, and always goloshes.

And if it all were to change under the eye of some sorcerer : if those down whiskers, that long nose, that raspberry-red blush and that smoothest of all olive-oil-smeared Stratilatov pate were to jump over on to some other quite unexhibit-like head—say the police inspector's—well, on to Zhiganovsky himself, and Zhiganovsky's moustachios on to the

Prefect, a little consumptive man who had through persistent illness ·irretrievably lost all his natural bounce, while Stratilatov were himself to change into some sort of whale, or a pig, or a mouse, or as a white swan soar away with a flock of swans over the Volga,—all the same you would not mistake him because of that little blue cornet paper bag and his goloshes.

In the court, as in the other government offices, the clerks usually drink tea co-operatively, and each member's sugar comes to seventeen copecks per month. According to Stratilatov's reckonings it was more profitable to take one's own sugar. That is why the little blue bag and Ivan Semyono-vitch are inseparable, and every one knows that. As for the goloshes, the Stratilatov pair would not give place in matter of hugeness even to those stuck out in Okhlopkov's shop window for gapers, and what is more, at the very first view you are struck by the circumstance that they are only put on for appearance: Stratilatov's high boots are welted soldiers' boots made of thick coarse leather that neither rain nor frost can get through, and alone, without assistance from any goloshes, they swallow up space beautifully.

Rising at six at the bells of All Saints and praying to God—and Ivan Semyonovitch prays at length and with passion—and shaving and having his growl at Agapevna, who since time immemorial serves in the Stratilatov house, after his morning

tea he sets off by Cat's Alley to the second-hand
market, where he jostles round all sorts of antiques
and bookstalls a full hour, just like a blind man in
his dark spectacles, rooting out as it were with his
nose the cast-aside treasure heaped as it fell muddled
among rubbish.

The antiques market was not for Stratilatov the
idle amusement of an idle man, the antiques market
for Stratilatov was very existence, his business, like
an epidemic for a doctor or a brawl for a lawyer or
an accident for a newspaper-man; and it was not
from his thirty roubles a month (or thirty-six pounds
a year) clerk's salary, but through this antiques
market that untouched in Stratilatov's name there
lay a whole ten thousand roubles (that is, a thousand
pounds) in the government bank.

'People with brains can always get on, fools
never!' that was what Stratilatov used to say.

It was while he was still young that Stratilatov
had taken to this trade, the sale of antiques. He
was always able to buy cheaply, and never went
to the stalls without his money-bag; and, while
others were gaping, he would snatch up the beloved
article,—no dilly-dallying, after which he would get
rid of it to the city buyers at a good price. In that
way, buying up and reselling, Stratilatov scraped
together his capital.

Our town is famous for its old things.

But not profit alone, passion too drove Ivan
Semyonovitch to the antique stalls; and not less

a passion than that of his neighbour Tarakteyev, the corn-merchant, a well-read fellow and a numismatist; and, for the sake of some engraving or other of quite doubtful quality (and certainly not a Rembrandt, to whom he liked without exception to ascribe all his engravings), he really would not have stopped at quarrelling with his friend as badly as the town doctor Likharev and the architect Baranov, who recently quarrelled for life about some chairs or other said to be Peter the Great; nor did Ivan Semyonovitch sell all the treasures he acquired, but kept some for himself, and of the really valuable ones. And that is why among the clerks of the court alone Boris Sergeitch Zimarev, the undersecretary and Stratilatov's immediate chief, earned Stratilatov's sincere respect and even friendship, for his ability accurately and faithfully to place antiquities.

In our little town everybody knows everything.

In his own way.

By nine Stratilatov is in the court. He comes first, before any one else, and it is only recently that Lykov the secretary is not behind him, indeed, sometimes forestalls him. But Lykov is an exception, and not in the least like preceding, real secretaries: Lykov is not afraid of the government attorney, and every one is afraid of the government attorney; and Lykov's tongue is not a clapper or a stinging shaft—but yet if you get on to it you would find it more comfortable in the devil's claws,

for he will make a laugh of you and rate you up and
down and rattle away straight before your face
without any of your roundabouts or equivocal
delicacies, nor lies nor flattery ; and when everybody bursts laughing not even his eyebrows twitch
—you would think they were clamped down under
key ; and he knows the laws as well as if he had
made them up himself.

Stratilatov does not come into the court empty-
handed ; as well as that little blue bag of sugar he
bears some ancient article from the stalls—a picture
or an icon or a book or some trifle. And his first
care is to lay the purchase behind his chair against
the glass cupboard where the forms and paper and
other office requisites are kept, and then, blowing
his nose so that the whole cupboard rings and the
other with the glass broken by Adrian Nikolaievitch
answers, and putting a clean sheet of paper under
each elbow in order not to dirty his sleeves, he sucks
at his pen and starts on his copying.

It is advisable not to disturb Stratilatov before
twelve o'clock ; at twelve o'clock the secretary asks
him for the work given the day before, and, willy-
nilly, it 's hand over the papers (and if you don't
hand them over, Lykov does not like to be indulgent,
he 'll spin such a stunner round you you wouldn't
know your own father).

And it is not so much the reproach as the failure
to obey in itself that terrifies Ivan Semyonovitch.
He is devoted to his superiors and full of awe before

them, and the higher a superior, or, as people say, any *personage of discernment*, the greater the awe; and his hamstrings tremble and his legs fall under the scythe and he gets the goose-flesh and a trembling pervades him to the point of tears, to complete paralysis of the reason, to complete forgetfulness of the most essential circumstances of life, such as *name, father's name, family name, age, sex,* and *position,* when, for example, he happens to fall into the president of the court, to whom he never said a word in his life, in the entrance hall. No, it is advisable not to disturb Ivan Semyonovitch.

But the very moment the secretary drives off to make his report and in his place all that remains is his table covered with papers, the most suitable time for a conversation with Stratilatov begins. He becomes inexhaustibly talkative; first one, then another, he gathers together all the clerks, and, whispering to himself from satisfaction, sets off on all sorts of terrible stories, all sorts of adventures, all sorts of historical events, contemporary events and apocryphical events borrowed from canonically repudiated books such as the *History of the Ark of Noah,*[1] and all of them, as if matched, extremely delicate in contents; he rattles away from memory as easily as reading from a book, basting it all with stories and jokes and observations on the way also of exceptional frivolity of meaning, and then he

[1] The story of Noah's Ark is recounted in 'The Fifth Pestilence,' page 69.

passes to verses better known in their manuscript form than from printed books, such as the famous *First Night*, and he declaims whole poems in a chant, just as in the theatre, the voice dying away.

What a laugh goes up! Why, you 'll burst, from laughing strain your loins, there 's no fence will stop him, no obstacle ; the three articled clerks at Stratilatov's table, and three at the opposite, Adrian Nikolaievitch's, Stratilatov's assistant, the clerk Zabalouiev, and Adrian Nikolaievitch the legless with his assistant, the clerk Koryavka ;— this one guffawing, that one sniffling, this one hoarsely whining, that one simply croaking, while Ivan Semyonovitch whinnies so that the dust rises and the grains show bright in the shafts of light, as if old papers long stored in the archives are being brought out and banged.

Any one else could not have held out, any one else would be suffocated, but as it happens just such an atmosphere as this has a beneficent effect upon Stratilatov : give him no bread, let him but fill his lungs.

His imagination warms up, more frisky and more frisky, more heady and more heady pour the words, and sometimes something comes out such that even the sky feels the heat.

Nor does he half whisper to himself any longer, it is as if he banged his cymbal, stretched, brave fellow, upwards on those wiry thin legs, ay, and all that belly a-tremble.

146

Sturdily thus will he stand open-pated to the sun, and that smooth, oil-rubbed pate, oilily blush like both cheeks, raspberry-red.

' Oh, the *Tinkling Cymbal and Sounding Brass* ! ' shouted legless Adrian Nikolaievitch, shaking from laughter.

When books confiscated on account, as it was put in the protocol, of their seductive nature, came for examination and destruction by the government attorney, Stratilatov, knowing the ropes, used to get hold of extremely—well, awkward works, and read them attentively line by line ; and, hooking out the most interesting passages, show them to the other clerks to the general satisfaction of the whole office, and he would whinny just as when he declaimed the *Rake's Alphabet*, A is for . . . or read the *Memoirs of a Widowed Priest*, which was really well-esteemed and quite popular ; and the dust in the same way would rise and the grains show bright in the shafts of light, as if old papers long stored in the archive were being brought out and banged.

' A filthy fellow ! ' that and nothing less was what the secretary used to say about Stratilatov, having in mind this way Stratilatov had of always pitching on the same subject.

Ivan Semyonovitch feared Lykov like fire, but to this opinion of himself he always turned a deaf ear ; it did not touch him, could not pierce his skin. Thank God, during his forty years of faultless service his nose had seen something or other, and

Lykov might well be a law-worm, might well, in fact, be as orderly as a German and keep every one else in fear and trembling—but all the same, and Ivan Semyonovitch would give his arm to be cut off on it, Lykov was a revolutionary.

Stratilatov did not admit revolutionaries to be people, but low rabble, making an exception of the Decembrists alone.

' Only the gentry can revolt, but these are all low rabble ! ' those are Stratilatov's actual words.

The young fellows, the clerks, who did not look so scornfully, severely, Lykov-like, on Stratilatov, used to make laugh of him and tease him when he was far from in a mood for laughter, most frequently in the busy hour before tea, while for their entertainments, and perhaps also because he would lend money, they even liked him.

Stratilatov's rule was well known to every one : ask him, and he won't refuse, and a receipt is not necessary, and only so that all should be in order when you return the loan he will ask you to sign, pull out of his pocket a sheet of paper folded in eight with notes on it and point to your name and say :

' Mark that it is received ! '

A wise rule appraised in its excellence by all.

And that is why when, at three o'clock when the crowd of young clerks poured out of the court, and, far from dignity, did so with great noise and japing, it meant that Stratilatov was leaving too.

On the way home he usually finished for his

escort some story begun in the court and that, by its delicacy, demanded great expressiveness,—only interrupting, and not in the least to the story's disadvantage, when he passed a church, as he considered it his duty without fail to pray as soon as he was level with a church, and Ivan Semyonovitch prays at length and with passion.

In this peaceful manner in merry company and pleasant converse would Stratilatov, the day's labours at their end, make his way to the church of All Saints.

Passing the apse of All Saints, surrounded by gravestones that came right up to his sitting-room window, he would turn aside into his yard, and, in importance, dignity, worthiness, pass down the little path as becomes a civil servant, and glance through his dark spectacles into the neighbouring windows of the police inspector and in advance gustate his dinner, the hot *pot-au-feu* long awaiting him in savoury perspiration in the stove behind the rose curtain where old woman Agapevna too for long awaits him, time after time fanning up the disobedient fat-bellied little nickel samovar (which was of that noble breed we call *the vase*) with one of Stratilatov's yellow boots. Finally, reaching the outhouse where old furniture and chests and piles of sacks were stored, he would again turn aside, urging his step at sight of the narrow little verandah and porch and the little rotted door, askew, battered, covered in felt and American cloth.

Whence came Stratilatov and how was not known to any certainty. His father was a serf—the steward of one of the big landowners of our province, who finally ruined himself—a certain Obernibessov; and his mother was also one of the Obernibessov household. But at the same time Ivan Semyonovitch himself, not without mysteriousness, used to proclaim that there wasn't even, well, enough of the serf in him to cover a brass farthing, and he was a nobleman's son, and, as—thus he would have it —a form of indisputable proof, also not without a mysterious air and obvious pleasure, he used to indicate *this area* (as he liked to express it)—his long nose which you can see three miles off.

Well, for that matter, no one did dispute it, no one in fact bothered about it; and even free-thinking Adrian Nikolaievitch had nothing against it, indeed, on the contrary, was for some reason or other specially interested, and when occasion arose considered it his duty to expound his own hypotheses as to the mysterious begetting of Stratilatov.

Adrian Nikolaievitch affirmed that *this area*— the Stratilatov nose—simply proved nothing; or, if it did prove anything, then exactly the opposite. Why, his most legitimate descent from a legal parent, the progeny of a simple mortal, was clear to the veriest fool, and it would be another matter if he had a birthmark or other such ornamentation;

but what about *another area* no less prominent—
that is to say, Stratilatov's shovel-like ears, sharpened
at the apex, most authentically the veriest acme of
bluest blood, Obernibessov blood, and if you want
a clue you must go to those ears and not the nose
at all.

Whether Ivan Semyonovitch was mistaken and
Adrian Nikolaievitch right, or, on the contrary,
Ivan Semyonovitch right and Adrian Nikolaievitch
mistaken, it was beyond human power to make
head or tail of such a matter, and the best thing
was to rely on both of them, believing one and the
other, the nose and the ears.

Stratilatov's childhood was spent in the old Obernibessov Manor, and it seems that he was educated
in a way that just fitted his mysterious begetting.

Confusedly and dully did Ivan Semyonovitch
recall his early years, but he would have it their
course was lofty and strange.

Why, his christening was extraordinary. They
did not christen him in the font, but *through the cap.*
And this came about through most exceptional
circumstances. That year the village flock was
without a shepherd, the priest had died, while Ivan
Semyonovitch was born in the winter and was a
weakling and it was impossible to drive with him
in that state thirty miles to the nearest parish.
They sent Yegor, the Obernibessov estate carpenter,
to the village for a priest. But the priest could not
come—it was the feast of his church. What was

to be done ? Well, this : the parson christened a fur cap and gave it to Yegor for him to put it on the babe as soon as he arrived, and no other christening would be necessary. Yegor hid the cap, and off he went, and galloped half the thirty miles and then pitched bang into a drifted hole—he had forgotten the name. He turned back and went straight to the priest, but the parson did not want to tell him the name. ' Give me,' he said, ' sixpence, and I 'll tell you.' Yegor gave him a shilling of the steward's money, and, overjoyed at getting the name, he turned there and then into a pub and had a drink and warmed himself up,—and lost the cap. It was a little old fur cap, scarce worth twopence, but he did not quite like to go back with empty hands. With the utmost difficulty he managed to get hold of some other old thing and hurried off to the house. They put it on to the babe and thus *through the cap* did they christen it. There 's a fine story !

He grew up a sharper and learned his three R's very early. He soon mastered them and could shoot from a gun ; and at an early age gained a passion for reading, and devoured much and divers, but mainly divine, writings, and he essayed to write himself and made verses. At the age of seventeen, on his father's death, he moved with his mother into the town, into the house of the deacon of All Saints, Prokopy. All sorts of treasures were brought from the village, and, perhaps, were a foundation for the collections of rarities for which

Ivan Semyonovitch was famous, and gave a start to his business.

Stratilatov himself never mentioned his legal father, and answered any questionings very unwillingly ; and never without a sort of bitter feeling of injury and even scorn in his voice,—and only because his father was a simple mouzhik. His mother he adored and waited on assiduously, and caressed, and pitied and cared for more than for himself, and he even almost prayed by her. You would not find a more exemplary and respectful son, and after her death he retained most touching memories of her ; and the mahogany bed with little bronze winged lions and garlands in which she slept stood under a dust cover in the stable, sacred.

' I don't regret anything for Mama,' Ivan Semyonovitch would relate, ' I knew for certain that she would die, but all the same I spent six roubles, eighty-seven copecks (fully 12s. 6d.) on medicines. I was so miserable. I was like a fish out of water. There was no one to pour out tea for.'

A year after his mother's death, having got over the first anniversary mass, Stratilatov married.

They used to say that on the marriage day, after the ceremony, when all the guests had departed, he spent the night alone locked in the sitting-room, and, praying incessantly, struggled with himself.

' Ivan, remember yourself ! Ivan, no backsliding ! '—as if Ivan Semyonovitch was reproaching himself, bridling himself, till morning light appear.

153

And the sun rose, and all the same he had back-slided, and for that very reason the following day from joy did he sing songs.

He had taken to himself a young and beautiful wife.

Glaphira Nikanorovna was quiet, and tender, and you would rarely hear a word from her, and her one care was for her Johnnikins, or Vanetchka, as she called him, and she was such an assiduous woman and at the same time so desirable that it was a joy to look at her, and she was old-fashioned, a tray in her hands, her feet shuffling up, her head bowed down, the sweet answering echo on her tongue—what more do you want?—live, like Adam, in paradise! and yet by the end of the second year Stratilatov was alone again.

It must be observed here that at about this time a new examining magistrate was appointed to our court—a young man, a merry fellow, a great joker, and although he was no relation of Stratilatov's his name was the same—Stratilatov.

Such tiresome coincidences will come about; a fellow lives quietly, disturbs nobody, everybody knows you and no one has anything scored against you, and then, pflump! one fine day some one suddenly appears with the same name as yourself and turns everything upside-down. There you are, yourself and not yourself, or not quite yourself, because there is another one;—and share your name with him you have to, and share all sorts of unpleasantnesses. And this very person with your name appears—not in some head-swirling phantastic sense—not as a result of indisposition and evil imagination,—but in the most live, tangible way possible, with a *birth certificate* and even with a government appointment.

And thereupon an accursed thought appears; well, what if this newcomer . . . is the real one . . . and you . . . an imitation ?

Ivan Semyonovitch lost himself in speculation and began to conceive and elaborate all sorts of propositions :—what did all this mean, and why had it come about, and was it not a sign, and who was the real one ? Was *he* Stratilatov, or that fellow, the examining magistrate, Stratilatov ? And, unable to decide anything concrete, he put himself on his guard.

Everything went smoothly and no misunderstanding occurred ; no confusion, no changeling substitution ; and by the New Year Ivan Semyonovitch was indeed ready to cast all apprehensions from his brain and establish once and for all time that he in all truth was the real Stratilatov and the examining magistrate the imitation. And then, just as if there was some evil power in it, something took him to the party the old deacon of the Church of the Intercession, Artemius, gave on his Saint's Day.

As always, the celebration of Artemius' Saint's Day was done in liquor and merriment. The house was chock-full of guests ; the host carried off his feet. There were a lot of young ladies and a lot of dainty meats. Stratilatov was in the best possible frame of mind, and filled his pockets full of dainties for his Glaphira Nikanorovna and philosophized with the Achitophel of the Nunnery of the Conception, Canon Father Pakhom,—pluming himself with his learning and employing choice words in his turns of speech, such things as This-said-person-to-wit-being, and Buskynges, and Cheuing and Polylerites and Anemolians and similar extravagances, in place and out of place. And during the camelious hopping, as Artemius said, the dances, that is, he made the company laugh with stories about Karapet Karapetovitch and his friend, about the superiority of modern languages over the ancient ones, about mother-wit, and about *I chew laces*, and other not less engaging incidents, and so even failed to observe that supper was served. And then during supper, in the midst of all sorts of jesting, when the guests began boasting one to another, he seemed to hear Glaphira Nikanorovna mentioned in a tipsy corner and began to listen,—and it was so : they were talking about her and in most ambiguous and unindifferent manner, and then some one said :

' Pfou, you blind chicken, what are you talking rubbish for, she 's eaten into Stratilatov up to the ears ; a bucket of cold water wouldn't get them apart.'

Ivan Semyonovitch dropped his fork. Like the

butt of an axe had this fallen on his bald pate. The wriggly examining magistrate stood out before his eyes, and he remembered all his premonitions, all his alarm; and his eyes swam so, his heart beat so, he would have bitten off his own tongue. Under the excuse of a sudden internal disturbance Ivan Semyonovitch crawled from the table, and rushed off breakneck home, capless.

How he got there he does not remember. Foaming, he burst into the house and flew straight at Glaphira Nikanorovna with his fists.

'Out of it, out of my house!'

While she, wakened from sleep, could make nothing of it.

'Where,' she says, 'am I to go?'

And he gets hold of her hair, so that hair stayed in his hand, and jerked her to the door and through the door, and then with his knee down the steps from the porch:

'To Stratilatov, that's where, to your dirty little whipper-snapper of a Stratilatov, and don't let me as much as smell you here.'

Thus he turned her out for neither rhyme nor reason, and hairless.

Afterwards Glaphira Nikanorovna herself told every one the story with all the details, complaining of her bitter, orphan lot. Ivan Semyonovitch kept silence, and don't mention it to him; he blocked up his ears whenever his wife was mentioned, he would not hear her name. And when (and this was quite recently) Adrian Nikolaievitch's assistant, the clerk Koryavka, passed in tipsiness to talk about unsuccessful marriages in general, and, although he did not mention the name, talked very transparently, Ivan Semyonovitch snatched at the inkpot and threw it at Koryavka. It did not hit him ; Ivan Semyonovitch aimed badly ; the inkpot thundered on the secretary's table and there is a black patch to this day. Which means that even after thirty years it still boiled and pricked him—that will show you what temptations can be like !

That very year the examining magistrate Stratilatov was moved to another post ; Glaphira Nikanorovna lived the remainder of her days with her mother, quiet and meek.

It was impossible to stay alone in the house, it was dull, it was not convenient, and there ought to be some one to keep an eye on things. Stratilatov did not establish his quiet family hearth ; his family life was not a success ; but still, though badly, his life had to be arranged. Thereupon Agapevna took up service with him, and in her old age, useful for nothing, her wage demands were quite acceptable —no pay at all, simply her food—and from that time she serves him, making no answer back or complaint, in faith and righteousness.

Ivan Semyonovitch is a remarkable man, and the house of the deacon of All Saints, in which his tranquil solitary days flow by, a special one.

The house is not large—there are two low-pitched rooms and a kitchen—and everywhere burn little holy lamps—a lampadka in the kitchen, a lampadka in the bedroom, and as many as two in the sitting-room, one in each of the front corners. · Ivan Semyonovitch likes to light the lampadkas himself; he does not trust Agapevna,—she is old, her hands shake, and whatever she picks up drops out of them again; and only on fast days, on Wednesday and Friday, when, after Agapevna's example, Ivan Semyonovitch takes of the holy oil on an empty stomach, is she permitted to clamber up on to the stool and take a teaspoonful out of the lampadka.

When you go through the hall, if, of course, you do not get hung up on the coffers and do not twist your neck, there will be the kitchen; on the left a cupboard; straight in front of you a Russian stove with a rose curtain; and on the right, along by the window, a bench; and in the middle the door into the bedroom. And everywhere, in all the corners, down by the stove, behind the cupboard and under the bench, there are piled stale crusts of bread. Why Agapevna needed to collect crusts of bread Heaven alone knows.

Poor old Agapevna! Ay, but how the old woman

tries, toils, and moils, gathers her last jaded energies, only to please the apple of her eye, Ivan Semyonovitch. She looks after him as a little child, and rather than let him be miserable she would willingly tell him a fairy story, but her memory is weak, worn down by the years; or she would sing him a song, but she has no voice; or what you like she would do,—would have danced, wound in figures of eight and whirled like a hurricane, turned herself inside-out, but her old legs do not obey her; she would put up with anything,—a coarse word, were it but from his sugared lips,—an angry look if only from his bright eyes. She would have accepted sudden death if only from his white hands; while if Stratilatov were to die she would cling to him, to the deceased, as to the relics of a saint, and not corruption but a sweet odour would she inhale from his stinking corpse; and, who knows, perhaps it would be made whole again, and some other innocent soul pay with health from her prayers. Upon my word, if Ivan Semyonovitch made Agapevna bark like a dog or crow like a cock the old thing would not murmur, but scream, bark like a mastiff, cry out like a cock—but all this made matters no better!

In former times the old woman used to bake meat pasties, but now she has grown weak and can do nothing, overlooks this and omits that, and forgets to do something else; and all that she does do is breed mice.

There is one good thing, and that is that Ivan

Semyonovitch is not exacting. He demands only this : that there should be a lot of everything and as fatly cooked as possible, but whether it 's a cockroach or a bayleaf floating in his soup is all the same to him. And another good thing is that he is a strict observer of the fasts, and keeps all four ; that is to say, Lent, and the Fast of Peter in midsummer, and the Lent preceding the Assumption, and Advent, and all the twelve Fridays, and on Wednesday and Friday in general, and he is even inclined to observe Mondays.

' Look here, old woman,' Ivan Semyonovitch often says, ' 'tis a little you do, but yet, you know, your board 's a big item.'

' Yes, batyoushka.'

' A big item.'

' Yes, batyoushka.'

' You might at least clean out this washing-basin.'

' Very well, batyoushka.'

On hot days, before lunch, Stratilatov, not so much against the heat as for his pleasure, used to take a shower-bath of well-water down by the kitchen garden. The kitchen garden was opposite the kitchen window in the church enclosure, and the well, too, was there.

Undressing in the kitchen to the skin, and supplying himself with pickled cucumbers, Ivan Semyonovitch climbs out of the kitchen window, and, going round the vegetable beds, takes up a stand under the laburnum tree. Agapevna climbs up on to the stool with the washing-basin, and the ablution commences. And all the time the water trickles over his well-soaked olive-oil-anointed pate Ivan Semyonovitch chews pickled cucumbers, believing that with their help the blood will not run to his head and the sun is not to be feared.

A precaution not entirely superfluous, for as it happens the sun in that very minute would halt in its course, raising its tipsy sultry eye, and, blazing, hang there directly above Ivan Semyonovitch, lost in admiration of him (and he, in very truth, was magnificent in all his glory with the pickled cucumber in his mouth), or else envying him, and for that matter the satisfaction experienced by Stratilatov was so immense that his shovel-like ears, rising to a point, used to shine with light.

But rarely, however, would the pleasure be enjoyed without unpleasant results, though not the sun (for the cucumber was protection against that) was the cause, but Agapevna. Either would the basin slip from her trembling hands, or she would pour the water wide of him, or she would souse herself or go rattling, basin and all, from the stool to the ground.

' You might at least practise a bit,' Ivan Semyonovitch would say, out of humour, ' you simply pour away the water for no purpose. You 'll be making another universal flood.'

And indeed, whether from devotedness or not daring to ignore his commands, or else from fear

162

of this universal flood, Agapevna did practise; she dragged the empty tub from under the cabbages and put it under the laburnum tree where Ivan Semyonovitch took his stand and then clambered on to the stool and poured away. But nothing of any use came from it all. The tub was showered in proper manner; but with Ivan Semyonovitch it would not work, and some time ago she almost broke his head with the basin.

' You 're a punishment to me, old woman ! ' Ivan Semyonovitch would often say.

' Yes, batyoushka.'

' My cross.'

' Yes, batyoushka.'

' You might at least let some air into the rooms, this isn't a postal-telegraph office.'

' Very well, batyoushka.'

Ivan Semyonovitch dines in the sitting-room.

Kitchen, bedroom, sitting-room, that is how the rooms go. The sitting-room is the principal room of state, and there does not seem to be a free nook in it anywhere, it is all filled up and hung in.

On the walls there are oil-paintings and engravings in huge old-fashioned frames, and water-colours, miniatures and Gobelins, and all the pictures and engravings are of beauties, and all of them, as if sorted to match, in their seductive natural state. There is one exception, the portraits of the Tsars. There are other pictures, but hung face turned to the wall, and these are the pictures where the ladies are absent. And so many beauties look from the walls that it is impossible at once to distinguish where the face is and where the *appurtenance*, but Stratilatov himself knows every little finger, every dimple, every mole, and most gladly gives explanations, expressing himself in his own peculiar fashion, in verse unpublished.

According to Ivan Semyonovitch's own words he would, were it possible, turn all the beauties into one penknife and place it in his pocket so they might be inseparable from his heart, or he would like to turn them into fine-dressed dolls in order to play with them, pressing them for ever to his bosom.

Then, the moment your senses return, after the pictures other objects step out before your eyes. On the left from the door is a huge chest brimful of books, and from the chest up the wall there goes a glass-fronted case of coins. The coins rest in rows on a green field, and are all rare and in fine condition, since all rubbed-down—blind—ones pass on mighty smartly to some amateur,—if to no one else then to his neighbour Tarakteyev. And from the case to the corner is a table with portfolios, and in the port-folios engravings all on copper—Stratilatov keeps no others—and, of course, all are Rembrandts. And, finally, in the corner, an image of the Saviour, *The Fearful and Terrible Salvation*. On the right from the door is a wot-not with Saxony china, and next the wot-not along the wall a table ; and on the table old caskets, miniatures and cheap seductive postcards ; and under the table a ponderous enough trunk as long as a man's outstretched arms full of silver and ornaments, and on two opposite sides of the table Viennese chairs, and fitted in the corner a mahogany cupboard. The cupboard is a special one of precious objects ; in it there are cups white as sugar with a monogram of ducat-gold, an ink-pot in the form of the imperial crown,—a gift from the High-School girl Yakovlyev whom, as Ivan Semyono-vitch himself admitted, he tried to seduce a whole three years in vain,—Stratilatov's seal, made in the form, as it were, of a finger dangling, round which was an inscription, *From* THIS *All Things Took Their Beginning* ; and, finally, little golden slippers and an ancient cup in the form of an egg on chick's legs with a golden wing in place of a handle. This cup Stratilatov lets no one touch, and cares for it more than his own eyes, because his mother drank her tea from it. On top of the cupboard is a current account book in which Ivan Semyonovitch enters and tots up every week his expenditure on alms to beggars, and on the doors of the cupboard is an ancient Obernibessov tie with tassels. In the corner is an image of the Mother of God—the Image of *The Solace of all the Suffering*, and between the cupboard and the image an old piece of arms.

But Stratilatov's pride is an oval mirror with oval concavities which reflects sixteen-fold.

' Buyers have prayed on their knees for it, offered me one hundred roubles, but I wasn't taking it ! '

boasted Ivan Semyonovitch, proud of his treasure not to be sold.

The mirror hangs between the windows that look on to the All Saints chapel surrounded with tombstones, and in front of the mirror is a table, with a chair at each side and an armchair with eagles in the middle.

In this place, in the imperial armchair between the two unextinguishable images of the Saviour and of the Mother of God, in front of the sacred miraculous mirror, Stratilatov takes his dinner.

When the meal is ended Ivan Semyonovitch will undress, take off his grey lustring jacket, pull off his great boots, kick them into a corner, and on to his side he goes. Stratilatov lies down; lies down Agapevna too.

The bedroom between the sitting-room and the kitchen is a passage room, and against the kitchen side wall is a couch, and next to the couch a rickety iron bedstead with an unshaken flock mattress and a pillow made greasy as a pancake. On the couch sleeps Agapevna, on the bed Ivan Semyonovitch.

Stratilatov sleeps tranquilly and undisturbedly. A healthy, deep sleep has wrapped him in its light wings, and it seems as if all circulation of blood has come to a stop in him, and, as the All Saints deacon, Prokopy, puts it, the *slumber common to all things* has begun.

Stratilatov dreams very rarely, but if a dream

docs come, then it is such a bad one that he might just as well have not lain down to sleep. Three dreams particularly troubled and vexed Stratilatov.

He dreamed he was in the ancient coach of the Empress Elizaveta Petrovna, wearing his jacket of grey lustring, with the imperial crown on his head and sitting as if rolling on deep pillows. Through the window flashed houses with monograms, and there was the same name everywhere, and that was his own name Stratilatov, and the people were running after the coach shouting ' Houra ! ' and there he was sitting magnificently rolling on his deep pillows, not thinking or desiring anything, in perfect bliss, houra, Stratilatov ! But then, just as the coach was turning on the bridge towards the old women's market, somebody's hand suddenly dragged him out through the window into the frosty air. There were no horses and they were harnessing him, Stratilatov, in the jacket of grey lustring with the imperial crown, to a three-hundredweight waggon-shaft, and ' Off you go ! Whip him up ! ' And Ivan Semyonovitch heaves and rubs on the three-hundredweight shaft, and bruises his whole side, and falls down, and gets up again and drags himself inside-out ; but that coach would not budge, not one bit. And an inexpressible fear fell on him and he began to yell and his yell came in a fading, piping voice.

Then another time he dreamed that he was sitting in his imperial armchair in front of the miraculous mirror, and, reflected sixteen-fold, was admiring himself, and suddenly noticed that his nose had twisted to one side and he was quite unrecognizable ; one nostril was tiny as the eye of a needle, and the other huge, wider than his fur hat, and through it he could see his throat. And again he cried out from horror.

The third dream was the most terrible, more terrible than either the coach or the nose. He dreamed that he was little again and his deceased mother was alive. It appeared his mother had not enough time, and pastry had to be made, pancakes cooked, and not simple, but proper ones such as at wakes. And there she put him into a box and covered it up tightly with a lid and carried it to the graveyard and there buried it in the ground. ' You 'll spend a night there, and in the morning I shall come for you ! ' and off she went. There he lies in the box, and there was no room, and he could not turn over, and his side hurt him, and the damp from the lid was dripping on to his face, and he could not wipe it away because he could not raise his hand. And the drops were cold and heavy, one fell on the bridge of his nose and ran down his nose and into his mouth, and another one after it. *Mother of God, O Virgin, rejoice,* Stratilatov wants to pronounce, but instead of the Mother of God he begins to recite from Pushkin's condemned and blasphemous poem the *Gavriliada :* ' *At sixteen years a guiltless resignation. . . .*' And in horror he yells and knows that the grave is deep, and no one can hear his voice and he is only shouting inside.

And all these fearful dreams for some reason or other he dreamed just before Twelfth Night,—on simple working days he ordinarily dreamed nothing at all. Tranquilly and undisturbedly sleeps Stratilatov. A healthy, deep sleep has wrapped him in its light wings, and it seems as if all circulation of blood has come to a stop, and, as the deacon of All Saints, Prokopy, puts it, the *slumber common to all things* has begun.

But there is not time for dreams in this after-dinner hour, and they begin their evening life while the daylight has still not gone.

To the left of the couch are bookshelves, and, disposed according to their importance, are the *Historical Magazine*, *The Russian Antiquarian*, *Old Russia*, and, right at the bottom, *The European Messenger* and *Russian Thought*. On the shelves in front of the books are snuff-boxes, and again cheap postcards of seductive beauties intermingled with views of holy places. Opposite the bed is a bookcase up to the door, over the door two oleographs, on one a nymph seated in a tree, on the other Seraphim of Sarov and the Bear. Then another bookcase and a chest of drawers with engravings (engravings on copper, and, of course, all Rembrandts), and in the same place all possible sorts of salutary little pictures with which the caretaker, Loukyan, is presented on Saturdays. Between the bookcase and the chest of drawers is a stand, and on the stand is a knight in plaster of Paris with a musket and armour.

Cunningly the beauties look from their postcards :

' Ivan Semyonovitch,' they wink at him, ' get up ! ' and they grin like little devils, all black-eyed, and the beauties provoke him, ' now come on, old bald pate, up you get ! ' Then, one after another, they cast down their eyes again like Nell the Gelding that lives in Denisikha.

And the nymph bends down from the tree and stretches out her tiny finger :

' Stratilatov, I have come ! '

And the holy fathers and forefathers, and great martyrs and just, and great miracle-workers, from their flaming timber huts and quiet cells come out with the bear and bless him :

' We shall be at thy right hand ! '

And the plaster of Paris knight with the musket and armour does not take away his staring white eyes.

In vain ! Ivan Semyonovitch sleeps with the sleep of the just and nothing will stir him, nothing touch him. And even if the terrible little blue volume itself, squeezed in in the corner of the bookcase between the *Repentance of the Hermit* and *Love—a Golden Book*, passing on one side the *Exploits of Ivan the Merchant's Son*, *The Estimable Housewife*, the poems of *Neledinsky-Meletsky*, *Batyoushkov*, *Polodinsky*, *Koltsov*, and *Nekrassov* and

other beloved books, and pushing way through
Tolstoy (hated by him) and Gogol (despised by him),
and Dostoyevsky (above the power of the mind),
and other similar authors, were to climb out of the
bookcase and open itself—the terrible GAVRILIADA,
that is to say, beloved and hated, sacred and accursed, why, even that would not rouse him from
his tranquil, undisturbed sleep.

The sunset dies down, all objects become uncertain
as if intoxicated ; and the wind brings the sound of
bells from old bell-towers. The ringing re-echoes
and confuses, bell answering bell, rising and falling,
festive, stormy, and droning ; and a wingèd, buoyant
swan-bell floats in from over the Volga. And
suddenly, like a great hammer coming down on
a cast-iron block, the chiming makes the world
tremble, ay, your temples throb. And no longer
is it a mere bell, but the voice of the Lord, driving
in the flock from the fields ; the bull roaring, the
mare whinnying, the moor-fowl crying, the thunder
rolling, the little bells clinking, the little bells
clanking ; and through all the roar and din a bird
shrieking in his ear, shrieking and shrieking. Lord,
what a stupid thing !

Exasperated, deafened by the shrieking, Stratilatov springs on to his feet, rubs his dull glued-up
eyes, and crosses himself—' Lord, I have called on
Thy name '—and, spitting at Agapevna, lost in a
world of snores, he again rolls over on to his warm,
crushed bed. ' I 'll have a few minutes more.'

And quietly and peacefully he sleeps with the sleep of the dead.

' You know, Boris Sergeyevitch,' Ivan Semyonovitch complained more than once to his friend Zimarev, ' my old woman Agapevna snores quite murderously, just like a sergeant-major. I can't bear it ; I am a light sleeper—the least sound. . . . And in any case cultivated people cannot suffer snoring.'

But what can you do ? There, even Zimarev himself, for all his being under-secretary and able to define any ancient thing—and he will tell you the day and month of its age too—even he is powerless against nature. You cannot get past nature !

' Old woman, you eat a lot of bread,' Ivan Semyonovitch would try.

' Yes, batyoushka.'

' It 's bread does it.'

' Yes, batyoushka.'

' People will be talking about me and I get a bad name. " Fine things he does ! " they will say.'

' Yes, batyoushka.'

' 'Twill be a sin for you—why, it 's a deadly sin. . . . You might restrain yourself a little.'

' Very well, batyoushka.'

And thereupon, either from devotedness or not daring to ignore his commands, or else from fear of deadly sin, the old woman tried to restrain herself. And for a minute or two she would somehow hold herself in half-way towards sin, but then afterwards how she would let herself go ! Such a snore, such a whistling ! The neighbour Tarakteyev has a house of stone, and even there it was audible !

Poor old Agapevna, both laughter and sin.

' I have decided to have done with Agapevna,' Stratilatov again complained to his friend Zimarev, the old woman has been up to falling off the stove ; she can't walk straight ; she climbed up on to the top, and then rolled off and nearly killed me, from that height.'

And, eternally complaining and swearing to the end of his life he would not keep Agapevna, Ivan Semyonovitch all the same could not imagine how he would part with the old woman. No, Agapevna had grown to the house. All the nooks and crannies knew Agapevna, and Agapevna knew everything her master, Ivan Semyonovitch, needed. To part with her was as difficult and, it seemed, as impossible as it would be difficult and impossible to leave the tiny low-pitched rooms of the deacon's house whence he had buried his mother, whence he himself had married, and where, after the fashion of all people, he desired in good time to render up his soul to God. And even if in temper, exasperated beyond measure and, perhaps, really offended, he drove her out, all the same on the second or third day he would infallibly pull himself together and go straight out into the dusk on the porch and call,

' Agapevna ! '

' Here I am, batyoushka ! '

THE boulevard is the place set apart for the promenading of all citizens. On the boulevard Stratilatov is at home. Whether there be hindrances or all go smoothly and evenly, all the same every day, when replete with after-dinner sleep till seven, at *seven* Ivan Semyonovitch sets forth to walk on the boulevard.

When he has braced himself in the fresh air he seats himself somewhere on a seat between the restaurant and the bandstand, and sits there sprawling as on those traitorous deep pillows in the golden coach of the Empress Elizaveta Petrovna; and he does not stir, he drowses a bit, whistles a bit, waving his stick before him, in pleasant expectation, with one single thought :—Is it not time to drink tea ?

Passers-by down the side path can see his grey jockey-cap with its button and his shovel-like ears rising to a point that quiver restlessly every time the rustle of a woman's gown can be heard.

It is not the same on Sundays, when the band plays in the evening on the boulevard. The music moves Stratilatov to tears, he falls ecstatic at the sound of it, and it seems he cannot sit quiet one minute more ; or if he sits down he jumps up again immediately. And what you will—cut his throat, even !—he will run to and fro. To the thought, *Is it not time to drink tea?* is united, excited in his incorrigible heart by the music, an unslakeable desire about which he will tell in the most touching moments of friendly confidences and which nothing you do can destroy,—the desire to find among all those promenaders such a young domestic maiden as would *love him disinterestedly*.

And he runs like a madman as if eyeless, in his dark spectacles, seeking somehow—is it not by his nose ?—in that gaily attired crowd flitting by, that one who shall *love him disinterestedly*,—calling to her, whispering to her to come.

When the dusk deepens, and the famous lamp hung waggishly on the rope between the bandstand and the restaurant is lit, the boulevard livens up. Noisily the town ragamuffins and loafers collect, and behind the noisy pack, at its very heels, enters something suspicious and scandalous ; and the boulevard takes on that Sunday evening air that gives promise of broken heads and the lock-up. Remarks of approval and disapproval begin to be uttered loudly and shamelessly, till you 'd really call the police. Here some young blood has thrown a lighted scrap of paper on to a young lady's knees and she has uttered a shriek as if her throat had been cut, and there another has pinched an unacquainted lady and there is another shriek. Shrieks and guffaws and giggles and jokes and apings and playing the fool.

Stratilatov elbows his way into the thick of it, and, surrounded by the young men, clerks and shopwalkers and the like, jokes away on his favourite theme ; and, in his fury reaching the extreme, he whinnies.

But even in his fury under the maddening, desperate music of the hoarse instruments, under the drunken cries from the restaurant, under the snatches of squeaky, wearisome couplets that come and go, like those that are sung in Russia year after year :

'This eclipse took place in the taverns,
This eclipse took place in the taverns . . .'

amid all this eclipse coming and going, and the most outrageous scandal flashing like a spark now here now there, Stratilatov even in this dark crowd seeks among the promenaders the maiden who may *love him disinterestedly*,—calling to her, whispering to her to come.

' I am a cavalier,' Stratilatov says about himself when on Monday people begin to pass through the court in connection with some incident of the boulevard, ' I should never permit myself, I am not a to-morrow's recruit on the razzle, I am not a whipper-snapper, a Zabalouiev son of Zabalouiev.'

When he has had enough of promenading on the boulevard Ivan Semyonovitch, at about ten o'clock, returns home to drink tea.

Stratilatov loves a cup of tea, and drinks a lot of it, taking his time, black as ink, and with Relly (or was it O'Reilly ?) jam, though more often with honey, with lime honey from the canonical honey-

176

combs of Father Pakhom. If a visitor happens to come, he is always glad to see him, and will offer him a cup, and produce cakes, and explain this, that, and the other, and show him the rarities; and full of *much favoureds* and *great honours*, lead him to the door. Visitors never sat long with Stratilatov; you 've had your tea and off you go.

Behind the samovar when it is time for the seventh-tea-sweat music appears. Stratilatov is a master on the guitar; yes, and sings too, although his voice, alas, is not of the first. But, however it may be, he sings with feeling, sense, and passion.

> ' I see thy black veil like a man insane,
> And misery rends my cold soul in twain . . .'

sings

Stratilatov, and the guitar ting-tings.

Agapevna listens with tender delight.

' Well, is it good ? '

' It is, batyoushka, so good, oh so good.'

' A-hah ! ! '

> ' Why does he follow me,
> Everywhere seek,
> But always so cunningly
> Look when we meet ? '

sings Ivan Semyonovitch,

and the guitar ting-tings.

Agapevna listens; moved to grief is the old woman, a tear breaks through, and she weeps.

' Well, is it good ? '

' Oh, so good, so good.'

' A-hah ! ! '

On weekdays Stratilatov sets but a little time
apart for singing—there is work on weekdays—
but on Sundays there is all the time you want both
before the promenade and after it.   And all day,
as if in joy, he sings songs.

Whether it is that Saturday puts things right
(and on Saturday, after standing through the
vespers without dropping in at his house, he sets
off for the boulevard and from the boulevard goes
to Denisikha—in Denisikha there are certain
houses of iniquity ;—and, after spending an hour or
two there he returns home and goes straight to
bed), or whether from some other cause known to
no man, on Sunday after the morning service
in the Prokopiev Monastery and late mass in the
Nunnery of the Conception there is no end to
his singing.   And if one must make a comparison let it be no offence to say that Ivan Semyonovitch pours forth like a real cock nightingale
and the whole house of the deacon rings with song
like a wood in Spring.   Unhindered, as if in answer
to an imperial decree, the song pierces the wall to
the inspector and circles like a swallow round the
tombstones of the Chapel of All Saints.

' Well, is it good ? '

' It is, batyoushka, so good, oh so good.'

' A—h-a-a-h-h ! ! ! '

*

Besides Agapevna, for a certain period an artist from Petersburg who could speak five languages, as he made known his own glory, was an unfailing auditor of Stratilatov's song-singing.

This Shabaldaiev (or the devil only knows what his real name was) appeared on the scene as unknown and unexpected as a bolt from the blue, and went straight from the harbour to Stratilatov. He praised his rare pieces and expressed amazement at his reading, and his taste and his grasp of things ; and so he fixed himself up. You can take towns by flattery ! But besides that, although God did not make a mock exactly of the artist, for he was well built, he had not taken any trouble about the rest—his appearance was not in the least artistic, he was even bald, pitiful—well, a miserable little pair of breeches—though, 'tis true, inclined to play the smart with his collars and his raspberry-coloured velvet waistcoat. But all his clothes were threadbare, you know, and torn, and under his arm he carried a portfolio with pictures.

The Russian is a fellow full of pity, and Ivan Semyonovitch's heart was touched. Whereas the other was a fox

' I,' says he, ' won't be in your way ; I will sleep on the bench, and stick my little tail under the bench, and my portfolio under the stove.'

And Ivan Semyonovitch let him spend the night. He spent the night, but once he was there he would not go away, drive him if you would with brooms. And thus he installed himself.

And he spent a week,—and another, and he fell into the ways of the household, put up with the ways of the household—a liar and a boaster, he would get round anything and make you look a fool. And such a scoundrel—why, he 'd crawl into your very ear, that 's the sort of artist he was !

Ivan Semyonovitch would go off to his office, and that fellow to slouch round the town, to paint pictures, he would say ; and, although he never held a brush in his hand—his portfolio held nothing but pictures cut out of the *Field*—he was nevertheless accepted as an artist.

The people about here are shy and careful how they go.

But, all the same, Stratilatov soon had enough of his tenant, and found great pleasure in getting him into clear water, and making fun of him.

For example, the artist boasted that he could speak five languages ; but boasting will not take towns—boasting is a trap, and it clapped to and there was an end to it ! Why, it turned out that he had not the least idea of either the ear or the snout, so to speak, of anything but his own silly gibberish. Although people speak truth when they say that you can get through the world on gibberish, whenever Ivan Semyonovitch put any question out of Russian history to him, say, in what year was the *Thief of Toushin* crowned, or asked him to recount all the *eunuch metropolitans* Russia had had,—he would begin wriggling, and however much he might refer to some Princess Konkratov or other, whose receptions, he averred, he frequented, and where he was quite at home, and to all his acquaintance with Petersburg notables, artists, and writers, he would have to bite his tongue in the end when Stratilatov got him thoroughly against the wall. And thereupon he ought to have been turned out head and tail foremost with his portfolio, yet Ivan Semyonovitch did not turn him out, but retained him in his house, finding great satisfaction in the instigation of disputes in which he was in a position to evince his superiority.

In a month or so Stratilatov had got to ' thou ' with him, and then cut his hair in all sorts of styles, beginning with the *pagan* like the pagan Saint Vladimir baptized, and the *convict*, when he cut the left half down without touching the right, or for a change leaving the left and shaving the right quite off, and going on to the *French*, when he copied a picture of some *Count de la Barthe* or other, or simply cutting him *à la Napoléon* ; and he always took him with him for his walk.

' I take you as a contrast,' Ivan Semyonovitch used to explain. ' The girls will look and compare us, see who 's the finer.'

The artist slept in the sitting-room on the chest, his portfolio under his head, his coat for coverlet, and in place of bedding Agapevna got some sort of padding things. Every night when he went to sleep Ivan Semyonovitch first crossed him, and then sent him on his way, always with the same words :

'Just you look out, you pea-headed fool, there are some books, you know, underneath you—but then you 're a weakling, who 'd take anything from you ? '

The artist lived with Stratilatov a whole year, accompanying his benefactor on his walks and listening to his singing. Just think what the man had come down to ! And there, somewhere in Petersburg, who knows, perhaps in very truth he worried his way into and imposed on those said notables, artists, and writers,—there are not a few fools on the face of the globe ! Yes, and moved in such society, and every one afraid of him ; but before Stratilatov he had folded himself in a sheep-skin. Ivan Semyonovitch got the idea into his head that the artist should address him in respect as nothing less than *the despot*—' Despot,' he should say, ' Ivan Semyonovitch'—and he did not even turn against this.

' Know thy own sin and madness, villain,' Stratilatov would say, ' I will subdue all thy five tongues.'

' Subdue them, Despot Ivan Semyonovitch, your will is law.'

' A dose of prison for thee, varlet, a dose of the dungeon ! '

' Dose me, Despot Ivan Semyonovitch, your will is law.'

' Thou 'lt rattle thy bells there, *scloundrel* ! '

To this too, to everything, the artist agreed.

Such obedience was very easily explained; why, whatever you say, thanks to Stratilatov the artist had free bed and board—a very important circumstance; and when in need you will do anything for this alone. Well, without a farthing in his pocket, where could he have gone, who would have let him into their house with his ridiculous portfolio? It is true that he had no bed of roses, but in these days a man will take anything at a pinch, though what if the portfolio did not contain pictures, but an explosive bomb, an *exploderous jelly*—nitroglycerine—concealed.

The people about here are shy and careful how they go.

Just as unexpectedly as this Shabaldaiev had appeared on the scene, so he disappeared suddenly. He pleased a member of the court—there was a funny little tippler a member of our court, named Prosvirnin, and he took a liking to the artist because he drank well and did not make you press him, and put down glass after glass without taking a bite between. They were drinking once at Berkhatov's and this member got dead drunk and fell in a heap on the floor, and began going on all fours, and simply could not get up though it might mean a night in the lock-up. The artist got him to his house and obtained a loan of one hundred roubles as gratitude, —and was no more. And however much they searched for him they could not find body or bones.

Stratilatov always remembered his tenant with pleasure, and was not in the least perturbed that his tenant was not an artist at all, as it transpired after inquiries, and not a detective, as he made himself out to the policemaster, Zhiganovsky, but in general a dark personage and withal a Turkish subject. It was all the same whether a Turkish subject or an artist, whether from Petersburg or from Riga, it was no matter, but really now there was no one under Stratilatov's hand except Agap-evna, to listen so attentively to his singing, and there was no one before whom it would be so easy to let himself go, with no resistance.

Not so long ago Ivan Stratilatov made friends with Yagodov the choirmaster, and things went very far, and he thought he might not remain among the living. He was scared out of his wits. He got his head in a noose, so to speak.

In no worse fashion than that artist, like a mass of snow on your head, Yagodov came down on our town, and put every one to confusion at once. His visiting-card, that passed through everybody's hands, produced a very great impression.

A. K. YAGODOV

Composer of Liturgical Chants
Sanctioned by the Most Holy
Synod Gold-medallist Etc. Etc.

What a card for you !

' That 's no joke,—sanctioned by the Most Holy Synod ? '

' He 's got five gold medals.'

' We 've got a man now ! '

' He 's brought twenty hundredweight of music alone ! '

This was the sort of talk at all the street corners. Every one was rubbing his hands with pleasure ; our people love liturgical chants and prize choir-masters.

Having done all the objects of note in the town, after the Monastery of the Intercession and the Nunnery of the Conception, after the boulevard and Berkhatov's Inn, the choirmaster dropped in to see Stratilatov. He appeared covered in medals, showed his visiting-card, and inflamed Ivan Sem-yonovitch. The guitar ting-tinged, and the singing commenced. Let this clever man try my voice, was Stratilatov's thought. And he was not mis-taken. The choirmaster listened attentively through a number of airs, and again, in order to make an impression, doubtless, showed his card, and patted Ivan Semyonovitch approvingly on the pate.

' Your voice is not a big one,' said the choirmaster, ' because you have not worked at developing the vocal chords ; you can sing second tenor.'

And from that time he was always trotting off to see Stratilatov, all, it was explained, to hear

the singing. He was not very anxious to listen,—
and what countless times even did he not beg for
it to stop,—but at the same time, under a plea of
the development of the vocal chords, he demanded
recompense. Ivan Semyonovitch, not a bit grace-
fully, all the same, did give the choirmaster twenty-
one copecks, just enough for a pint of vodka if you
take your own jug ; and then began to wriggle out
of it and at last absolutely refused. But the whole
misfortune of the visits of the choirmaster lay not
in this. Pfff ! as for that recompensation, why,
rarely enough—well, once a month, perhaps—Ivan
Semyonovitch would give his sixpence—he was not
going to ruin himself ;—but this was the matter :—
the choirmaster brought him to shameful confusion
every time with his talk, and led him towards sin.

On one of the first of the choirmaster's visits
Stratilatov, unfolding before his visitor all his
learning, started talking about Pushkin. The
choirmaster could only remember out of all the
poems ' The Bird,' but that not Pushkin's, no, one
he had sung while still at school,—' Oh, little birdie,
stay ! ' and that only half-way through, which he
did not omit open-heartedly to confess. And all
this seemed to fit in just right. Why, that was
exactly what Stratilatov needed ! Anxious to show
his superiority, he fastened on Pushkin and recited
a lot of verse, and all, as he himself put it, *of an
erotic characterization.*

' Pushkin,' Ivan Semyonovitch said in conclusion,

' was a fine man, but he ruined his soul with the *Gavriliada*.'

Now it is quite true that a word is not a sparrow : when it jumps out you cannot catch it again. Ivan Semyonovitch had spoken about the *Gavriliada*, and over-stepped the mark. For some obscure reason the choirmaster got interested, began to ask questions, and, having learned the essence of the *Gavriliada* (the seduction of the Virgin in turn by God's Ambassador Gabriel and God Himself and finally by Satan, all in the course of one night, which led to the disastrous uncertainty of the initiated as to the paternity of the Son of God ; and to the bewildered but intense gratification of the Virgin herself), he clung on with both hands, a knife at Stratilatov's throat ; let him copy it. Not wishing to enter into any petty wrangling—why, not only to discuss but even to think of the *Gavriliada* did Stratilatov fear—he pulled the terrible little blue booklet from the bookcase and handed it over, only in order to get out of the frying-pan. He handed it over and simply found himself in the fire. Into the trap and can't get out ! Not only did the choirmaster copy the *Gavriliada*, but he learned it off by heart to the last comma ; and then he was off, every time he saw Ivan Semyonovitch, reciting line after line from memory. He would come in the evening to take tea, but as soon as he had a glass in his hand off he went, and though he might hang up once or twice, all the same, word for

word, letter for letter, out it came. Ivan Semyonovitch did not know what to do, what means to try,—
it was simply beyond all patience ; and it threw
him into a heat, and his sweat broke out, and he
wriggled on his seat, but there really was nothing
to be done ; he 'd started the tune, so to speak,
and now he had to pay the piper.

' I say, choirmaster,' Ivan Semyonovitch would
try to defend himself, ' you would be roasted alive
for this. That 's what would be done to you, like
as Ivan the Terrible roasted Prince Vorotynsky,
that 's what. Or is there really no God in you ? '

While that worthy jabbers away—hisses away,
may he vanish in the eternal fire !

And, having racked the *Gavriliada* through and
through, he set out on philosophic meditations and
again stirred up such a stench that it was really a
little too much. There was the *Gavriliada* wouldn't
get out of your head while the same head split
from philosophy.

How many evenings did not the choirmaster
drive Ivan Semyonovitch to the point of madness
with the question of *the fourth person of the Trinity*,
and the possibility of its fulfilment,

———how shall this thing come to pass ?

Or about some council of the twelve emperors
who look for justice and the law buried in some sort
of cairn *near the field of Poltava*, and when they dig
up the law and justice they will present *boots* free
to every one but all made on the same last and

every one obliged to wear them although they
don't fit—

 —how shall this thing come to pass ?
Or of some *fowl's word*, which, if you know it,
 —all shall be possible for thee.
And finally, of the approaching comet, the tail of
which is to touch the earth and in a few half-minutes
 —all shall perish that be, verily man and
 beast.

' But what about the Judgment Day ! You are
lying,' Ivan Semyonovitch resists. ' Do you think
you ought to ? That 's not very prudent ! '

' Without any Judgment Days, in half a minute,'
the choirmaster persists, ' from the gases.'

' From what gases ? ' springs up horror-stricken
Ivan Semyonovitch.

' From the gases,' the choirmaster keeps on.
' You won't be able to hide anywhere, and all will
die drunk without wine, mad without mind, man and
beast together, and in the whole wide world *alone
couch-grass remain.*'

Well, and how would not a man be confused ?
The comet was within bounds, the philosophizing
used to be worse, if only when about that Sheesheega's awful tail, and Yagodov averred the
Sheesheega would cover you with its tail and you be
lost, and however much every one looks for you they
can't find you and you can't find yourself either ;
else when about some obligatory universal and
withal artificial interment like *the Australian*, and

189

everything somehow broken off, hazy, obscure, incomprehensible, and what is more, contrary to the faith—how then not fall into sin ?

A mere chance alone rescued Stratilatov from misfortune. In the central church under Yagodov's direction girls from the High School took part, and there after two or three general choral meetings a complaint arrived at the ecclesiastical offices that the choirmaster behaved in an uncomposerlike manner with the schoolgirls. The office ordered an inquiry and after the feasts dismissed Yagodov *for slackness*. Making use of the incident Ivan Semyonovitch broke off relationship with his friend. The reason was most suitable ; both this said slackness and the fact that quite another inscription appeared on the choirmaster's visiting-card :

A. K. YAGODOV

Onetime Choirmaster of
a Rotten Choir.

This choirmaster became worse than any comet for Ivan Stratilatov—you regret even friendship in the end—for he never had a good word for his friend. And better let them all be enemies and you alone stay amid the couch-grass, to such a point was Ivan Semyonovitch in despair.

But the heart is not made of stone, and at the last

minute a friend was again found—Zimarev, Boris Sergeyevitch, assistant secretary. This new friendship sprang up from quite different impulses ; there could be no question of showing his superiority over his friend, and singing remained quite on one side. According to Stratilatov's conviction the choirmaster and the artist were not a bit up to Zimarev's level. In the first place Zimarev was his direct chief and his defender against Lykov the secretary ; in the second place he had such a knowledge of antiquities that he could poke any connoisseur in the waistcoat ; and, finally, he would not put up with Stratilatov's extravagances and would not enter into such diverse conversations, as if his ears were hung with gold and everything had to be done sensibly and in a business-like manner, even to the extreme.

He was wizened and little, without a hair on his head, and when he walked his left foot bounced up, and when he sat down with Ivan Semyonovitch and they both buried themselves in some old manuscript or made out an icon their ears coincided—Zimarev's ears were the merest trifle smaller than Stratilatov's.

Stratilatov was full of respect for his new friend, prizing in him his superior and a learned man and a very modest fellow, and he used to take his advice and pour forth his worries, and although the other would have made him a grandson he looked on him as a contemporary, as a man getting on, made wise by long experience,—in a word, he saw his equal in

191

him ; badly preserved, 'tis true, but all the same of equal years.

Zimarev (but not as an example to other visitors) was supposed to sit a while ; and after tea he was given tasty, really filling bread too, not bread such as others got, the sort you don't want to swallow, real brick,—and all sorts of rolls and cornets and mouldless jam ; and Stratilatov has a great stock of jam, and when a jar goes mouldy the mould is scraped off and his visitors have that pot.

In course of time Zimarev, like to the artist and the choirmaster, became, by the natural course of things, one of the unfailing auditors of Stratilatov's song-singing.

' Singing is a great matter,' Ivan Semyonovitch used to say, as if justifying himself for his passion before his severe silent friend who did not utter even a mouse's squeak. ' It is impossible for one person to sing, it 's sad singing alone, Boris Sergeyevitch.'

Generally in the evening after his walk, and when he has drunk his tea and played on the guitar, Stratilatov sits down behind a book and reads for an hour. Historical reading and poetry is more to his mind in his solitude than stories and novels, of which he knows so many that really there is nothing left to read. His favourite poets are Nekrassov and Koltsov, but he places the poet to whom Fet gave his *quivering torch* above them all,— it is he whom he considers the universal poet.

'Yes, and a blueblood too, you know!' Ivan Semyonovitch explains, getting up with a little bow every time from excess of respect.

Exactly after one hour the book closes, and is placed accurately on its shelf or in the bookcase in its place, and the lamp is put out. When he has prayed earnestly for coming sleep before the *Fearful and Terrible Salvation*, and before the Virgin, *The Solace of all the Suffering*, and growled at Agapevna to keep the screw down, Stratilatov lies down to sleep, concluding thus with prayer and growling his solitary laborious day.

'Well, you know, I am not just like any one else,' Ivan Semyonovitch likes to say, both to himself as he sweetly stretches under the coverlet, and to his acquaintances by daylight in the office—'like any one who goes to an inn. And just you see how much I have read; how many antiquarian pieces I have collected; and my faultless service. I succeed both there and here; the Sheesheega will not cover me with its tail, I shall not be lost, because I am a good man!'

And when he talked in this fashion Ivan Semyonovitch was not boasting in the least, and any one who knew the least bit about it was ready to sign with both hands that in all truth the Sheesheega would not cover him with its tail and that he was a good man. Every one had said much the same about him, and only one single time that merchant Tarakteyev the numismatist, who had made friends with Zimarev out of numismatic interests, a man of sense and not a fool to let a coin go by, said something not very flattering about his neighbour ; and on Zimarev's objection that Stratilatov too was a human being, said with a laugh :

' Not really ? ' and laughed again, ' and I thought it was the Missing Link.'

THE present Spring turned out a special one; Stratilatov's sacred dream of a quiet family hearth for himself was nearing realization. It seemed to Stratilatov he had found that young domestic maiden whom he pictured whenever in Denisikha he took painted Nell the Gelding by the hand, and who listened to him when to the accompaniment of the guitar he poured forth more fluently than a nightingale, and looked at him from all his post-cards, old portraits and engravings, and whom he sought as on the boulevard in the evening he pushed his way hither and thither through the noisy crowd of promenaders. It seemed she was found at last, the unattainable, unapproachable, unimaginable one who would *love him disinterestedly*.

No, whatever you may say, the old man had not gone off his head. He merely felt everything in him renew itself, brace itself; in place of a raspberry-coloured pate dark curls such as compress a maiden's heart puffed in the air; and his eyes turned blue, and he became almost like Emelyan Prokoudin the policeman,—you know, a well-set-up, dignified sort of fellow with a pale face and red lips; and all he lacked was spurs.

When he went out in the morning at his usual hour, without knowing why himself, Stratilatov felt a sudden joy; whether because melting snow was dripping from the roof and there were daws chatter-

ing there and the wall of the Chapel of All Saints
had grown dark; or because the deacon Prokopy
went across to the church quite lightly clad only in
his under-cassock, with his scarf wound round his
neck and his fur cap jammed on his head simply
from habit; and a woman ran by with a cowl-staff
and buckets to the church well only in her one
garment and goatskin shoes, and a hen wandered
about clucking ' Where, oh where, can I lay my egg ? '
—or was it all on account of that above-mentioned
policeman Emelyan Prokoudin who went by with
rattling spurs to the inspector ? Everything pleased
him and he wanted every one to be pleased. He
paused at Tarakteyev's stone house with the high
steps to the porch in order to take breath; and such
a desire came on him to make his neighbour a present
of some rare gold piece—say, one of the double
ducats of Peter, why not ?—only at once, this very
minute. . . .

' Oh Lord, Master of my life, preserve me from
despondency and the Spirit of Idleness and love of
vain power and speculation and idle talk ! ' Ivan
Semyonovitch whispered the great Lenten prayer
of St. Ephraim the Just of Syria, as he cut through
Cat's Alley on his way to the bric-à-brac stalls.

Stratilatov made his appearance in the court at
his usual hour, and this day he brought many and
diverse articles from the antiques market. His
haul of curios had been a most successful one.

Snatching away a minute from his copying, he

thrust his hand behind his chair ; and, pulling from out of the heap of purchases piled there a number of dainty little objects, laid them on the table in front of Zimarev, while out of his side pocket he pulled a little copper triptych and placed on the top.

' There is a maiden of a good family ; your advice would not be in the way,' whispered Stratilatov through his dried lips, bending to his neighbour's very ear.

Zimarev took a sideways glance at the row of objects. The ruddy copper of the triptych flashed in his eyes and his spectacles suddenly bedimmed.

' Boris Sergeyevitch, you 're a sound man, and getting on in years, too, be a good fellow and advise me. She is called Nadiezhda, and lives with Artemius the old deacon of the Prokopiev Monastery, she 's his niece.'

While that worthy, nodding his head, ran his thin fingers all over the triptych and turned it over and over, and put it so near his nose it looked as if he was smelling it all over.

' And the deacon drinks,' went on Ivan Semyonovitch. ' Often drops down during the service ; and she is a thin, pale little thing, truly an orphan, as you will see for yourself.'

' That 's so, that 's so, indeed ! ' and Zimarev simply gulped from satisfaction, for he has been touched on a raw spot. The triptych was just such a rarity as he had been exerting himself to get a long time, and had looked everywhere for—it was

our Russian Nicholas bareheaded with a tiny church
in one hand and a sword in the other, *Nikola
Mozhaisky*.

' She 's of good family, the deacon's niece. . . .
She 's nowhere to go, a poor, pale little thing . . .'
and Stratilatov rose from his chair and in his agita-
tion began to stroke his bald head; and for a
minute it seemed as if he might suddenly do something perhaps extremely unsuitable, such as have
a stroke or lose his wits and crawl on to the table.

' Golgotha ! ' Adrian Nikolaievitch suddenly
shouted out, pointing at him with his hairy finger.

And the same thing that usually happened whenever Lykov the secretary for some reason or other
was late now took place; jeers and jokes began to
pour on Stratilatov from all sides and stupid smart
phrases, ba-ba-ba.

' Holla there, you nose of a general ! ' somebody
squeaked out from behind a typewriter.

' Nikola Dupliansky ! ' or as one might say, ' St.
George of Whittleborough ! ' was returned from
the counter.

' Demurrage ! ' capped the legless one.

' How 's your god getting on, how 's the old man's
health ? ' returned Zabalouiev the clerk.

' He 's caught a chill, you can see,' giggled the
articled clerk who sat next to Zimarev.

' He 's eaten some goose and got a tickling in his
throat,' let out Koryavka.

' I know, I saw Ivan Semyonovitch on the boulevard with two young ladies,' broke in the other articled clerk from Adrian Nikolaievitch's table.

'Tinkling cymbal and sounding brass!' nodded Zabalouiev.

And many more still of such thrustings and jabbings did Stratilatov get; but, deep again in his copying, listened with the tips of his ears alone and did not even snarl as he usually did on such occasions, did not utter his customary 'I ask you to get on with your work!' and even his pate did not flash its usual red.

Adrian Nikolaievitch, who was famed for the composition of letters of application that never failed to have results (since from birth, there can be no doubt, he was destined to occupy himself with such an art), brought some important document to a conclusion, and, sticking his lumpy red beard out in front of him, he began to read it for the edification of all.

A petition by itself alone magnificent came to a magnificent conclusion.

'For Xenia Fyodorovna Piskounov,' read the legless one, mouthing and smacking over every word, 'For Xenia Fyodorovna Piskounov, illiterate and most obedient subject, Adrian Nikolaievitch Hrenov, Chief of Table, has most subjectly signed and with the deepest emotion I most humbly solicit condescension for my miserable family consisting hereby in conclusion in I myself.'

'Myself,' mocked Koryavka. Koryavka's tongue

always seems to be in pickle, and altogether he is a sodden fellow with his head in an eternal gloom of obfuscation, ' I, I, I myself,' and he went through the pantomime of signing.

But Adrian Nikolaievitch, raising his hairy finger menacingly, cried out in a fury of passion :

' Arise, on your feet, O drunken Russ debauched, and take to Your embrace those that be hostile ! . . .' and, shoving away the assistant, he screwed the application up tightly so that the parchment crackled, and then fell into that benign intoxicated state which usually ended so unbenignly.

Everything in the office was immediately hushed and the scraping of the pens grew very faint as if afraid to break the happy minute that promised so much amusement.

Supporting his grey head by his hand the legless one began to chant his favourite rebel song, the song of Vanka Kayin, and sang it in a bandit rebel way, his voice audacious, unbridled and stormy :

' O mother greenwood, stir not thy noisy leaves ;
Peace to a fine lad, to me, to think my thought,
To-morrow, O my mother, before the court I go . . .'

' sober, tranquil family hearth, . . . a poor, pale little thing, an orphan, without any home,' whispered Ivan Semyonovitch to Zimarev, sucking his steel pen as if it were a spoon full of honey and observing nothing, seeing only her, thin, pale little thing ; and he felt and was ready for anything. His heart was stirred by the song ; let her suck his heart from his body and dry his body up. . . .

And when Lykov the secretary appeared, and with the help of one-eyed Loukyan the caretaker and Gorbounov, Adrian Nikolaievitch was, without cessation of his singing, locked in the archives cupboard and there, in an ecstasy of world-grief, yelled the cupboard down and then began to sob and blubber like a child, with pitiful expostulations that life was wearying and he was sick of it, Ivan Semyonovitch for once melted and felt sorry for the legless one.

‘ It ’s no use knocking your head against the wall, Boris Sergeyevitch ! ’ he suddenly burst out in a loud voice (meaning Lykov the wall), a thing he would never have permitted himself if the minute had not been so full of feeling.

‘ By the Trinity Saint Sergius, down there by Moscow town,
     Stood a new and noisome j-a-i-l . . .
Where a bold brave fellow a prisoner lay, in right sore sorry plight,
     But his heart did never f-a-i-l . . .’

                  the legless one tearfully howled.

Whereupon the last grain of patience broke, burst, in every one ; and some one snorted and they all began giggling and laughing one at the other.

Lykov was the only one not to laugh.

‘ Be so good as to go on copying ! ’ he said, going

round the tables and putting a pile of papers in front of every one ; the key of the archives cupboard hanging on his little finger.

Stratilatov, too, who usually liked to laugh at the legless one, did not laugh, and not because that time had gone, but evidently because such was the moment.

And at tea also on that remarkable day he proved unusual ; he had the custom of treating the clerks with sugar out of his own little blue bag and unrestrainedly would jabber all sorts of balderistic balderdash like a prayer, somehow ecstatically pronouncing his beloved little words with a sort of tender love, just as if it were the word of God or the magnificent titles of high personages. His whole nature was filled to overflowing.

' Oh Lord, Master of my life, preserve me from despondency and the Spirit of Idleness and love of vain power and speculation and idle talk ! ' would Ivan Semyonovitch whisper the great Lenten prayer of St. Ephraim the Just of Syria, in sudden haste at the most interesting passages, when again he would set off jabbering still more balderistically.

His whole nature was filled to overflowing.

Stratilatov had seen Nadiezhda, the object of his love, for the first time at the celebration of the Saint's Day of Artemius, the old deacon of the Prokopiev Monastery. Sweeter than honey and sugar did she seem to him.

' Such a young thing—sixteen years—and slight,

but when they began to sit down for supper, she disposed herself—and half the sofa did she take up ; on her finger a silver ring with a turquoise, the crooling little dove ! ' thus did Ivan Semyonovitch report his first impression later.

All the evening he did not take his eyes off her, kept seating himself beside her, making her laugh by his stories, and when they played postman's knock he only called her out, and in forfeits when a troika had to be made up she of her accord picked him.

They met on the boulevard, for Nadiezhda worked at the costumier Elena Antonovna's and used to promenade every Sunday on the boulevard with the other master-hands, and he used to walk with her. Both the Summer and the Autumn, and the whole Winter too he courted her.

Further and further, and the fire got to the hay, she became as dear to him as the steam of the bath-house. He was beside himself, quite unlike himself ; and as for sleeping, he no longer could as he should, but kept turning about—stifling it is to him who loves—she alone was in his thoughts, she alone he understood ; about her alone was he in constant delirium :

' My little dove, my crooling little dove ! '

*

Now Agapevna introduced a cat on the sly. She taught the cat to spend the night under his bed to induce sleep. As soon as Ivan Semyonovitch lies down out from under the stove does she drive poor Tom and puts him under the bed.

But Tom is such a growler, and sets up his song *forking and raking the hay in the making*—and, well ? —sleep, no ! Ivan Semyonovitch tosses about . . . stifling it is to him who loves—she alone in his thoughts, she alone in his understanding ; about her alone he is in constant delirium.

' My little dove, my crooling little dove ! '

And what is worse, when he learned about the cat he roused a whole tempest :

' I don't want to sleep,' he said, ' to that sort of tune ! I 'm not a sucking babe with your *raking the hay in the making* ! If I see that cat I wring its neck on the spot. It 'll make the whole house stink.'

And, in very fact, in that short interval of time Tom did leave a trace behind, and spoiled all the covers of the *Russian Thought* and the *European Magazine*, and, wandering about the heights, even touched the expenses book and one or two of the beauties.

Agapevna submitted, and tied up Tom's eyes, and carried him to an empty yard, and there left him.

But the matter went from bad to worse, and the days became disgusting. Yesterday's *pot-au-feu* or kasha third time heated would be better. At night Ivan Semyonovitch began to imagine he had not one, but two heads, that his neck had branched out into two weeny necks, on each of which nodded a head. Love, upon my word, drives to madness !

And at night he groaned like a bear, so you would have thought of calling the priest for the extreme unction.

'Why do you groan so, batyoushka?' Agapevna would call out.

'No, old woman; I'll take a turn in the yard and it will all pass over.'

And he would go out into the yard and straight to the laburnum tree—the laburnum tree is over by the tombstones—and climb up on to it and then begin letting himself down from the top head first. Love, upon my word, drives to madness! And at night he groaned like a bear, so you would have thought of calling the priest for the extreme unction.

His heart aches, his bosom is full of sadness, she alone is in his thoughts, she alone does he understand, about her alone is his constant delirium:

'My little dove, my crooling little dove!'

Agapevna was full of fear, and smoked him with incense on the sly, full of apprehension lest a sin be committed and the Sheesheega steal up and cover him with its tail and he lay hands on himself. But God was gracious and all went smoothly.

Twas in the very butter-week in comes Elena Antonovna, as it were, to see Agapevna; and, at tea, praised Ivan Semyonovitch to the skies for his fine looks and exemplariness, for his humble restrained manner of life, and then went on to talk about Artemius the drunkard and the orphan his niece, without any home of her own.

'What sense is there, Ivan Semyonovitch, in your spending all your born days alone,' Elena Antonovna gurgled in his ear. 'You're still a young fellow, and living like that with old Agapevna toadstools have sprung up in the corners. You should take Nadyorka now, she's at least a young sunbeam.'

Elena Antonovna's proposal suited Stratilatov's heart and hand; but decide at once on such a step he could not. At the same time his heart was full of impatience, and he was overjoyed and he was deadly afraid,—doubts had sprung up and he was not quite sure.

'Such a young thing—sixteen years—and slight; but when they began to sit down for supper she disposed herself—and half the sofa did she take up; on her finger a silver ring with a turquoise, the crooling little dove!'—and Stratilatov argued within himself; and no, he was not quite sure.

For the first week Ivan Semyonovitch fasted; and, after having taken of holy communion on the Saturday, he sent Agapevna as a scout to examine the niece. There was no point in putting the matter off any longer. He had thought about it enough, and he was decided.

Agapevna went on her scouting expedition and returned with pleasing news.

'But mighty fine! She walks like a peacock, she talks like a swan!' Agapevna praised Nadiezhda like a gypsy his nag, and, adding oil to the fire, she fixed Ivan Semyonovitch in a decision from which there was no going back.

There was but one stumbling-block—Nadiezhda herself. How would she regard Stratilatov's proposal, and would she consent to move into the house of the deacon of the Church of All Saints, Prokopy ? Elena Antonovna undertook to settle this last but not trifling matter.

But Elena Antonovna had not undertaken such a terrible piece of work ; and there, by the beginning of the third week in Lent, everything had been settled most satisfactorily and without any difficulties, as if by clockwork.

On Wednesday, a day memorable for all concerned, Ivan Semyonovitch admitted the thing to Zimarev and sealed his admission there and then by the presentation of that rare triptych of Saint Nikola Mozhaisky ; and on Friday, as he showed his friend some little antiquity from the antiquities market, he told him, bending down, as usual, to his very ear, and making his voice as business-like as ever possible :

' Nadiezhda has consented ; she 's coming to-day ! ' and, unable to contain his feelings, spread out into such a peacock's tail, so to speak, that even Lykov, collecting papers, smiled.

No, whatever you may say, the old man had not gone off his head. He only felt that he could not sit out to the end in that long, low-pitched, smoke-blackened office. There behind that large, knife-

jagged table was no place for him ; but far away—
in the open, where he was soon to be—with a river,
and the laburnums by the banks rustle, and in the
marshes the waves of land rise dark and birds fly.
And for the first time in all his forty years' faultless
service, on the excuse of a sudden internal upset
he left the court twenty-three minutes before time ;
and what is more, from overflow of feelings he re-
ported those twenty-three minutes not only to
Zimarev, which, if you like, was only proper, but
also to the clerks Koryavka and Zabalouiev, and to the
caretakers, Loukyan the one-eyed and Gorbounov.

From the court Stratilatov turned, not to the right
down Cat's Alley, but to the left along Intercession
Street, to the savings bank, and then, having de-
posited six hundred roubles in Nadiezhda's name,
returned home with a lightened heart. His huge
and heavy goloshes swallowed up space in fathoms.
He flew along as fast as his legs would carry him, so
that not only the devil, even a bird could not have
caught him. His thin wiry legs burned and his
variegated handkerchief stuck up like an ear—and
every moment he dragged it out and wiped his face.
Nimbly springing up the porch steps, he thumped
a solid thump on the door with his fist ; and without
taking breath thumped again and thumped yet a
third time—a flock of sparrows was sitting in the
yard, and he frightened them away.

' Who is it, batyoushka, who is it ? ' shuffled old
Agapevna behind the door.

' I, old woman, open the door.'

He was all aflame from impatience, and everything went with a rush; and Ivan Semyonovitch dined as if catching a train, with his watch in his hand. Elena Antonovna had promised to bring Nadiezhda towards evening, and it was already darkening. Nor did he lie down for his nap.

The white swan, never yet wounded, never yet blood-sullied, alive shall be there in his hands; and how he will caress it and pity it!

' M-a-a-a-ny, m-a-a-a-ny years! ' muttered Stratilatov into his own nose.

Yes, and he wouldn't have slept, in all probability. The rickety iron bedstead was no more, that morning Agapevna had carried it away into the outhouse. In its place stood a wide mahogany bed with little winged bronze lions and garlands, and in place of the crushed flock mattress rose one of springs,—it is true a second-hand one, but for all that as good as new ;—and a downy red quilt and a mountain of white pillows.

The white swan, never yet wounded, never yet blood-sullied, alive shall be there in his hands, and how he will caress it and pity it!

' M-a-a-a-ny, m-a-a-a-ny years! ' muttered Stratilatov through his nose.

Everything had been spring-cleaned and washed just as for Christmas or Easter; the dust wiped from the pictures and the cobwebs taken down, and you would think there was not one little spider left in the whole house. Those preparations had taken more than a day,—a month, more likely.

In the sitting-room the white table covered with a white damask-linen cloth with a round brass tray of tarts and cakes from Kositchkin's and Khaminov's, and gingerbreads from Tchouprakov's ; and there beside the Stratilatov cup on the gilded grid that contained a good two glasses—the sacred cup, an egg on chick's legs with a gold wing in place of handle.

Agapevna was fussing in the kitchen, managing the bellied nickeled samovar ; and Stratilatov's yellow high boot whooped from the pressure of air.

Ivan Semyonovitch put the holy lamps right, pulled the case of silver on to the chest of books, put the savings-bank book into the case—six hundred roubles ;—and he panted and puffed, and he opened the red cupboard and stuffed away that seal into his pocket—*From* THIS *All Things Took Their Beginning,*—and carefully took out the little golden slippers, and, sitting up to the table in the imperial armchair quietly began turning them over and over on his knees, just as if smoothing them on to the little foot, so disobedient, so spirited, the little golden slippers.

Say what you want, he will give you anything ! He will make presents, and with body, blood, and life will be your guard for eternity. Say but what you want, and he will be your eternal, faithful servant. Oh, white swan nor wounded nor blood-sullied; oh, white swan!

'M-a-a-ny, m-a-a-a-ny years!' Stratilatov muttered through his nose.

His subdued little room, though washed, though scoured, though free from all spiders, became closer and closer to him. It became stifling as in a spider's nest. Impatience throttled, like the rage that cannot be set aside, the sword that cannot be thwarted, the fire that cannot be extinguished; and his heart, breasting wave after wave, buoyant and irrepressible, cried aloud and afar. . . .

And outside the Spring evening was already blue; the crosses of the All Saints Church showed dark on the melting snow; the faithful corby sat black on a cross. Two rays from the holy lamps—from the Saviour and from the Virgin—meeting on the gold of the little slippers, flamed like a purple star.

His whole being grew strong and grew firm and like a strong tree in a strong storm thrust firmly its iron roots into the bowels of the earth,—and in him was the bone of old heroes.

Did he remember something, did his foot slip, did his heart suddenly throb? He let fall the slippers and rose, and, thrusting his huge fingers into the pockets of his waistcoat, stared forward at himself in his mirror like a blind man in his dark spectacles; and, reflected sixteen times, he smiled—and so smiled that a large white tooth in the corner of his mouth flamed out—worse than the weariness of death. . . .

> ' at sixteen years a guiltless resignation,
> and coal-black brows; beneath the linen shift
> resilient stirring of two virgin hills. . . .'

he whispered, not taking breath, line after line of the terrible blue booklet; and the two rays of the holy lamps, from the Saviour and from the Virgin, meeting on his head, flamed like a purple star.

And suddenly as if some one had struck him with all their might, frowning and ducking his head, Ivan Semyonovitch sat down on his haunches and there behind his bald pate sixteenfold peered Agapevna.

The old woman let pass a tear. The verse had moved her heart like singing; and she wept:

' Oh, how good, batyoushka, how wonderful!'

And for long Ivan Semyonovitch made no response, it had taken his breath away; and for long he could not open his eyes. Shaking his head limply and shielding himself he rose up more evil than a serpent.

' Old woman,' he suddenly croaked as if in the noose, ' out of my sight, out of my sight! Outside the house in twenty-four hours!'

Submissively, lowly, Agapevna bowed down.

The tears dried up.

' Good-bye, batyoushka!' and off she went.

You cannot hide the stitches in the sack. However hard Stratilatov tried to conceal the happy transformation in his life, and however cunning he was, it soon became common property.

The whole yard rejoices when a swarm is taken, the whole field when the flowers open, the stackyard when the flails get to work, and man when he is happy! You can tell a falcon by the way it flies. Ivan Semyonovitch admitted this himself.

Holy week came, and the fast was broken; and at that time every one knew that the niece of the old deacon of the Church of the Intercession Artemius, Nadiezhda, was living with Stratilatov, and that they were living in a perfect, though illegal, connubial state; and he calls her *his little turkey-hen-capon*, and she him, *my little cherub*.

They began to congratulate in place and out of place and in terms which, though carefully selected and respectful, were not quite convenient; and when the secretary Lykov was not there they used to put the most Stratilatovian questions possible concerning his felicitous family life and those felicitous details of it which it is usually considered unpleasant and, moreover, indecent, to touch upon.

The clerks came from all departments of the court, in crowds and singly, some to giggle, others simply to take a look; and they even came from the archives, and every one knows that only archivitical people work in the archives. The interest was so great, and it so occupied everybody that not only all the rules, but even all sorts of exceptions of decent conduct were forgotten.

At first Stratilatov warded it off by jokes; then he got annoyed and stubborn; then he lost his temper and began to wrangle. And, according to his rather indistinct explanation, the affair was quite different. In his tale Nadiezhda had taken up quarters in his house merely in place of Agapevna and for no other reason whatsoever; he had long been considering turning out Agapevna for all sorts of evil designs,—she had bred toadstools in the corners and snored like a sergeant-major; and she was stuffy-odoured and she coughed;—and some story about a cat Tom she had brought in to send him to sleep by its *hay in the making*. But *he* wasn't just like every one else, and not a bit like that *blasbeliever* the clerk Zabalouiev; and for that reason would never allow himself to behave so immorally, so badly, towards the orphan niece of the deacon Artemius—she was only sixteen and had no home. And all those who have such filthy ideas about him had simply made it all up out of their own filthy thoughts.

'You're striped swine, and nothing better!' Ivan Semyonovitch would conclude, and sweat pour in showers from his pate.

But absolutely no good came of all these explanations that ended with the striped swine, and he only stepped finally into the mire. They made a real mock of him :—why, there were all the clues.

Every day on his way home from the court he went into Kositchkin's or Khaminov's or Tchouprakov's and bought·supplies of cakes and sweets and gingerbreads which he never allowed himself in former times ; and on Saturday after vespers he no longer showed himself either on the boulevard or in Denisikha, which excited the intense displeasure of that particular Nell the Gelding ; and on Sunday he left the boulevard while it was still light and never waited for the march of dismissal. Finally, the mahogany bedstead with the little bronze lions and garlands that now took the place of his old rickety iron one, and the tender, simply paradisal, tea-drinkings on the verandah with Nadiezhda, that confused and made even Zabalouiev blush,—whereas Zabalouiev, as is known, has learned *bon ton* and fine manners and the way of the world and dancing no more or less than in that same location of iniquity, Denisikha. What will you say now ?

The incident which took place on the day of Ivan Semyonovitch's angel, John the Baptist—his conflict with the deacon of All Saints, Prokopy—would have opened the eyes of a blind man. While this conflict arose from a mere trifle.

No church has such a large congregation as All Saints after late Mass. People swarm up in a wave —no end to them—just as when they elevate the miraculous image of Theodore Stratilat in the Prokopiev Monastery,—you can't push your way through. Large numbers of people drive up, and not only the townspeople, but from the outskirts and even from distant villages. There is a crush in the church, and they stand in the porch, too, and in the churchyard by the well near Stratilatov's garden ; and there is not a little jostling.

The church of All Saints is one of the old *daily* churches as they are called, built by the parish (the folk-moot, that is), in twenty-four hours in fulfilment of an oath after the plague had passed ; and the service is a long one, the singing good, Father Mikhey a fine fellow, fiery and beautiful of speech, and his belly rises higher than his nose when he intones on the rising scale. The mad girl Sister Matrena is the attraction.

There are people not a mite good-looking, with most ordinary faces ; but they only have to smile and all their features become beautiful, and when you look at them you feel relieved, merry. Or a quite unnoticeable fellow comes into the room, but when he begins to talk, and moreover the simplest, most ordinary things, he suddenly seems to grow immense, and his words make you feel big and at ease. And others who only have to look at you and you feel relieved and merry. Well, that particular joy of which smile, speech, or look is full must be what attracts. The people follow such beings.

The mad girl is not exactly a girl—she is thirty

if a day,—but her little face is that of a child, and when she frowns she reminds you of a wild animal, —a squirrel, that's it. She wears bright-coloured dresses, bright red, or canary yellow, or punch; and a warm kerchief on her head, a downy grey one with black circles; and when she lowers it she quite disappears in it and you shiver.

While the Mass is still in progress she comes into the churchyard and sits on a stone next the well, and the people follow her. They surround her; this one crossing himself and that putting a penny on the stone, bowing, and taking up his position again, and another one standing fixedly staring. They wait. She sits on the stone; her eyes are bright;—why, it really is so, any little beast, any bird, the sun, a shower, the stars, the moon would start a tender conversation with her, as will little children.

'Sisterkin!' a voice suddenly calls from the crowd.

And she begins to talk out of breath, stumbling along from some great joy you would say, just as children do; now hurrying, now dragging it out, now confused, but every word lightens the heart so that it seems grass and stone and water must feel better.

She talks from the lives of the saints and the gospel, she loves talking about the birth of Christ, how the star led the Magii; when the Magii slept the star slept.

' Do not oversleep your star ! Or maybe there is no longer a star ? '

' We see, sister ! '

' Help us, sister ! '

' There it is, sister ! '

Then she will start the story of the goat—that was always hungry and however much you feed it it is always hungry ; and of the cock, how the fox tried to entice it by peas, only for the cock to look out of the window, and the peas were nice to eat, and the fox's teeth were sharp ; and again about the goat, how it ran after the maple leaf, all sideways, half-skinned ; and about the sort of people who half-skinned the goat—mockers and scoffers that the yardman will sweep up like dead leaves and tip into a hole ; and again about the cock, the fox deceived it with the peas and carried it away and ate it ; and suddenly about rivers running full to the banks and powerful, bright as silver, and noisy, and no sand or roots or stone can restrain them ; and about birds, what sort of birds . . . doves. . . .'

' The rivers are flowing, sister ! '

' The dove-birds, sister ! '

' Thou art our own, sister ! '

And again about the goat ; an old, old woman takes it out to pasture, and the old woman does not know what to do ; she has too little to eat and the goat is always hungry.

' I can't feed you, and there you are hungry.'

' We are not hungry, sister.'

' I haven't even enough spoons . . .' and she herself looks and smiles, and a scarlet blush covers the pallor and all is well, so much that it seems that grass and stone and water must feel better.

' Thank thee, sister ! '

' Do not leave us, sister ! '

' Thou art our own, sister ! '

Stratilatov was returning from late mass. On the day of his saint he considered it more fitting to pray at Saint John the Baptist, and not at the Conception ; and he was in a most birthday frame of mind. Pushing his way through the crowd he took up a stand not far from the stone.

The fool had already finished her stories and people were beginning to go away ; and she was sitting as unmovable as the stone with firmly closed eyes and suddenly fell like a stone on to the ground. Some one ran for water to give her to drink, but every one knew she was playing the fool and pretending, and would thrash about and groan until the deacon Prokopy brought her the water.

' A real idiot's nature,' said a squint-eyed man in a sheepskin cloak.

' You ought to be stoned, you accursed ! ' came from the other side of the crowd.

' The old woman sat on the tom-cat and rode off to see the parson. . . . Many happy returns, Ivan Semyonovitch ! ' The assistant-surgeon Zhokhov, a friend of Zabalouiev, passing by with some girls, winked across.

Ivan Semyonovitch nodded at the assistant-surgeon, eyeing the fool kindly.

And when the deacon with a vessel of water appeared she rose from the ground as if nothing had happened and drank thirstily, and began frowning, desperately, you know, wrinkling up her nose so that every one looking at her screwed up their noses too.

' And whom, Matrena,' the deacon's wife pushed her way forward, ' did you see in your sleep ? '

' The deacon.'

' And what, my dear, was he doing ? '

' I saw him,' the fool half chanted ; and then suddenly veiled herself in her downy grey kerchief with the black circles. ' I saw him . . . as if we were together, bathing. . . .'

A burst of guffawing interrupted the words. The deacon roared his loudest ; the deaconess uttered a squeal.

' There are such low creatures,' Stratilatov said with loathing, ' that have no respect for their spiritual rank ' ; and he spat and made for his garden.

' And your Nadyorka is a bitching little draggle-tail ! ' the deacon let out, laughing after him. He had got warmed up to that extent.

' Now, deacon, I 'll shoot you for that ! ' Ivan Semyonovitch turned round and slipped like an eel through the garden into the house.

Meanwhile the laughter grew no less ; the fool's

dream and Stratilatov's threat had brought it to fury point ; and a woman possessed of a devil began to yell.

But Ivan Semyonovitch kept no one waiting, and suddenly appeared as if sprung from the ground, with a huge Georgian pistol ornate with fine filigree. He stepped straight up to the deacon and five paces away halted, raised the pistol and began to aim.

And that instant dead silence fell. Only the woman possessed of the devil still yelled.

' Remember, O Lord, King David and all his mercy ! ' the old women whispered, sliding away like blind puppies from their mother.

' You 'd better try shooting out of a stick, it 'd probably be truer ! ' the deacon made a face at Stratilatov as if mocking his aiming, and began to draw back.

But Ivan Semyonovitch aimed steadily ; and it seemed that any moment he might squeeze the trigger, the shot ring out, and an end to the deacon.

The deacon suddenly shook all over ; and, sticking out his tongue, half squatting as if his little legs had given way, set off with his tongue lolling.

Thus the deacon disappeared behind the crosses surrounding the All Saints church, and only a few people remained about the stone ; some village women with bundles and the woman with the devil together with them, lying now flat on the grass, and smart Miss Spitsyn, daughter of Spitsyn the merchant, who looked after the fool ; and the fool herself.

She was sitting on the stone holding her kerchief on her knees weeping silently like children from whom a toy has been taken.

But Ivan Semyonovitch still stood and aimed. And without doubt he would have stood thus petrified with the pistol till evening, till night, if Nadiezhda's voice had not awakened him. Nadiezhda, hanging out of the window, was shouting at the top of her voice that it was time to come and drink tea —the cake was baked.

'The scoundrel, the mop-headed cur!' Ivan Semyonovitch came to, and went towards the house, with difficulty dragging his huge goloshes along.

Oh ay, in former times, in Obernibessov times, in those early years when his mother was still alive, how gaily namedays passed! Haysel came on; the sharp scythe fell and swished through the succulent grass, they cocked the hay and he would lie down beside a cock or ride ahorse and the horse rear up, champing and stamping. As many trees as there were in the wood, as many twigs on each tree, as many green leaves on each twig, he would know them all, ride the forest through and through.

But that is all over now; we sing another tune. The feast has turned out not at all festive.

The next day, after the conflict, on his stale birthday, as we would say, Stratilatov moved into new rooms in the house of his neighbour Tarakteyev, in the stone house with the high verandah-porch.

222

He did not want to leave his rooms.   It was hard, but he had to.   He did not want to move the things from their places, but he had to.   Nadiezhda simply went mad and like a wild beast shouted all down Cat's Alley that she would not stay one day in the deacon's spider's nest which was no place for her—the deacon had insulted her.   And she tore and tossed about, and in her feverishness knocked down the precious cup with the golden wing, and rushed at Ivan Semyonovitch in a fury, and began thumping him and banging him about the head and pinched him to bruises, and became so stormy, so impossible,—any moment she might have torn his eyes out.   Tie her up, indeed !   And so, to please Nadiezhda, Ivan Semyonovitch left the old house of the deacon.

The removal to new rooms, and the whole unfortunate story about the shooting of the deacon of All Saints, called forth fresh talk ; and there was no end to the chatter and jokes and jeers.   People said that no one had shot out of Stratilatov's pistol for quite two hundred years, and that it was impossible to load a Georgian pistol of that sort,—it would burst without the powder even ; and they made great fun of the deacon who took to his heels at the sight of a firearm, and said that the fool Matrena did not love her deacon any more after that.   And it was with particular satisfaction and sufficient plainness of speech that people related the details of the removal ; how the policeman

Emelyan Prokoudin helped to carry the furniture, and what reward he received for his zeal.

'Golgotha!' cried Adrian Nikolaievitch, pointing at Stratilatov with a hairy finger, 'thou cuckoo pate!'

But Ivan Semyonovitch was utterly uninterested in these cries, soaked as he was in the ordering of his new nook, he could only think of where to put the things, which seemed very numerous and somehow disobedient. All jeering and pointed questions rebounded from him like peas from a wall. Would he have admitted in the end that he was living with Nadiezhda not in the least like brother with sister (and of course that was what everybody wanted, his admission of the fact); or, entirely out of patience, would have had recourse to his inkpot and blackened the whole floor of the office with spots; or perhaps, armed to the very teeth, have taken again to his pistol—but this time, of course, the most rapid repeater there was—there was no point in considering. It all cleared up of its own accord.

Just as chance on a certain occasion saved Ivan Semyonovitch from the choirmaster Yagodov and the choirmaster's perditious incursions and Yagodovian God-barren philosophy, so on this occasion he was relieved, though not by one, but by a whole series of events, and of such importance that they drew the whole town.

THE Nunnery of the Conception comes next to the ancient Prokopiev, or *Procopius'* Monastery. In its past are counted not a few meritorious accomplishments and a great number of curious stories. It had saved us from enemies and sown the seeds of enlightenment, and captives had died within its walls in confinement,—both simple mortals and such that at mention of their name Stratilatov would invariably rise in reverence ;—and there was a time when the Khlysts with their ecstatic promiscuous rites of copulation flourished in it. But all these magnificences long long ago had grown up with fable, and the nunnery fallen into decay ; and ordinary domestic, snarling—monastic—life run its course.

But as early as the end of last year people suddenly began to talk about the nunnery, whispering ear to ear, audible corner to corner. The word went round that something extraordinary was taking place in the nunnery, and what is more, something of such a nature that even to think of it was terrible.

To the effect, in short, that at night a noise arises and the foul and unclean appears—harmful insects, marsh toads, stinking dogs, bats, scorpions, and all species of loathsome amphibia from which groans and cries proceed throughout the cells. But that is not all ;—to the effect that in the refectory all the articles for no apparent cause acquire the quality of ambulation, and the crockery falls from the shelves and the pestle flies from the mortar—ay, and if you begin gaping it will warm your crown for you !—and hot coals spring from the stove.

The Canon of the Conception, Father Pakhom—Achitophel—ran away from fear when, entering the refectory to read prayers, he saw a huge empty high-boot progressing towards him ; and a flying basket struck the deacon such a blow in the back that his kidneys were bruised and by Easter he expired.

And then it became known that quite recently some one had taken the nuns' name very much in vain, and that this dispensation could be only explained as a *temptation by fire* supposed to attack the nuns in the night and from which there was no escape.

Our police inspector Zhiganovsky, who loved to call himself Pontius Pilate, a courageous, straightforward fellow, having found out all about the truth of the matter through special subordinates, decided to deal with it in his own way.

And the matter was not entirely innocent. It transpired that the foul and the unclean, all those loathsome amphibia appearing, were nothing more than a fable set loose as a red herring, while the boot that progressed and the basket that flew were but skilful stratagems :—as a matter of fact the nuns at night lowered baskets from the nunnery walls and in them drew up to their cells their *cavaliers*, whereupon there followed the said *temptation by fire*.

The idea that possessed the police inspector was to burst suddenly in on them and put them to rout; and every one knows that Zhiganovsky sleeps two hours in the twenty-four and all the scoundrels have given in to him.

As usual, without long meditation, he went one night unexpectedly to the nunnery wall and sat in a basket and successfully began the ascent. And there in the basket twirling his dashing moustachios he drew whole pictures in his ·imagination of how amazed they would all be, and what a hurly-burly would ensue; what a fight and a scrimmage and a rout. And there at the very top, when all he had to do was to climb out and act, the nuns looked into the basket and recognized, horrified, the police inspector, and scattered like rooks, and squawked from fear, and let the rope go; and down went the basket and Zhiganovsky with it and so from that height crash on to the ground, and there and then he met his death.

The heroic end of Zhiganovsky became a tale leaping from tongue to tongue and no one talked of anything else. And *all wept lamentably for him*, as Ivan Semyonovitch, relating the event, put it.

There had not been time for the forty days' requiem to be sung when there was another event that made no less a stir in the neighbourhood.

Strastoterptsev (which is, being interpreted, Passionopatienson), a clerk in the court archives, who stood no lower than Stratilatov in his passion

227

for tea, made a bet, while killing time one evening in Berkhatov's inn with the clerk Predtechensky, that he would drink fifty cups of tea at a sitting.

Predtechensky accepted the bet, and they clasped hands and ordered tea. The ONETIME CHOIRMASTER OF A ROTTEN CHOIR, as he used to introduce himself, Yagodov, who happened to be at the next table, and his bosom pal the accordion-player Molodtsev, were summoned as witnesses. The Onetime Choirmaster poured out the tea, and the accordion-player marked it down.

And Strastoterptsev drank thirty-nine cups without a quack, and he tipped the fortieth down too, and had already started on the forty-first and got the saucer to his lips and begun to blow because it was too hot when suddenly water burst from his ears and mouth and nose—from all his openings, in fact;—and he stumbled and his eyes started, and he fell, and thus *water, water, everywhere* he left this world.

And a little after Strastoterptsev's funeral a thing happened such that, as Ivan Semyonovitch said, the like had not happened since the crow turned black.

In broad daylight the schoolgirl Verbov, carrying out the local revolutionary committee's orders, shot, by mistake, instead of the governor, a half-pay colonel Auritsky, and that very night Lykov was arrested and escorted by heavy guard to Petersburg.

And who would think of caring a damn about Stratilatov after this! And what was Stratilatov now ? Certainly very much *the missing link* ; no more. So the whole place would have answered in unison.

They had finished with Stratilatov, forgotten Stratilatov, left all his doings in peace ; and whether Nadiezhda lived with him or there never was any Nadiezhda in this world was all so far away, so unimportant and fundamentally uninteresting.

Ivan Semyonovitch felt as well as man can—no more sorrows ;—and happily and harmless will his life flow. The affair of Strastoterptsev did not touch him in the least ; indeed, may even be said to have excited a slight feeling of scorn.

' Why, it was simply a case of suicide by drowning. He drowned in himself ; God punished him for his thirst,' was Ivan Semyonovitch's comment.

He inscribed the police inspector Zhiganovsky on his list to be remembered in prayers next to *the deposed King of Portugal*, and he bought a candle for the half-pay colonel Auritsky.

At the same time he was in triumph now that Lykov was finally arrested—the incorruptible, adamantine Lykov, who raised his head about the government attorney himself and very nearly knew *that fowl's word* which, if you know it, you can do everything ! Why, Ivan Semyonovitch was the first to point out that Lykov was a revolutionary ; and if he did not talk about his discovery openly, but only in whispers when he confessed to Father Mikhey, this was only from respect and fear of superiors. Whatever you say, Lykov was a secretary, a superior, and of no small rank.

It soon transpired that Lykov was accused of organizing armed revolt. Ivan Semyonovitch, having nothing against this, added with satisfaction : ' and of expropriation.'

According to his observations it was not for nothing that Lykov used to go down past the savings bank.

' Of course,' Ivan Semyonovitch would say ; ' he wanted to rob it.'

Whereas time went on its course, without Lykov as with Lykov, paying no attention to who was right or wrong, where the mistake, where not.

Autumn arrived. The days were warm and clear —the earth dry, and the nights warm and quiet— full of stars. It remained warm up to the Birth of the Virgin, but after this Indian Summer the weather became damp, with rains.

Stratilatov began commercial negotiations with the object of acquiring a winter coat. He had decided to mark his new life by a sign, and re-attire himself ; and, having taken a fancy to a raccoon skin, he tried to tell every one about this purchase and have his lament about the general increase in prices. But no one paid any attention to his jabberings, and even Zimarev, filling the duty of secretary and proving a worthy successor to Lykov, behaved somehow in an unfriendly way.

Lykov's fortune occupied the whole office. Lykov

was the one topic. All possible suggestions were made; and as new data were acquired his further fate was decided; and what his bearing at the trial would be like, and would such a fellow let himself be hung if they sentence him as they did the schoolgirl Verbov.

So with all this talk and business nobody was amazed or even the least bit curious when, one fine day, just after the Elevation of the Cross, Stratilatov did not appear in the office. Three days his place was vacant, and only then was it noticed. Inquiries were made, and it appeared that no notice of absence had arrived. What was this about?

Zimarev set straight off from the court to make inquiries. He knocked at Tarakteyev's new rooms in the stone house, but Stratilatov was not there and there was no one to inquire of. Tarakteyev's little grandchild, a stupid, wooden-headed little girl, could only say that she was called Katie.

Having got nothing out of the little girl, Zimarev went to the old flat, hoping to find out something from the police inspector. But he had no need to meet the inspector, because he met Agapevna on the porch.

'Oh, it's you, my golden one,' the old woman rejoiced. 'But my old man, my old man,' and her toothless mouth quivered.

She took him into the house, made him sit in the sitting-room in the imperial armchair in front of the wonderful mirror.

Everything was in its place to the least trifle, just as if Ivan Semyonovitch had never even thought of moving from the nest he sat in so many years. The lamps were burning in the two front corners before the Saviour and before the Virgin, and the pictures too hung there each in its place ; and on the mahogany cupboard lay the day-book for the entry of alms, and on its doors gay the wonderful Obernibessov tie with tassels. The old woman had put everything just as it was in the old days, except that on the chest of books on which the artist had once slept sat a bewhiskered smoky cat, and, licking its whiskers, sang its *hay in the making* ; and that there was no Ivan Semyonovitch.

From inquiries it became clear what a misfortune had befallen Stratilatov. Why even those beings with seven· lives come at last to misfortune, alas, alas !

After her banishment Agapevna took shelter in the corner in the ante-room between the chests ; and, essaying to keep out of sight, somehow or other made shift. And then, when Ivan Semyonovitch moved to Tarakteyev's house, the old man Tarakteyev allowed her to fix herself up in the kitchen at the door—and look after the little granddaughter during the day. The old woman, for that matter, would have squeezed into a crack like a beetle, only not to part with Ivan Semyonovitch. The old woman felt there would be trouble. There was not one day without the policeman Emelyan Prokoudin.

Both day and night he was prowling around—he 'd a taste for other people's goods ;—and he beguiled his time in chatter with Nadiezhda. And people speak truly when they say :

> 'Sheep like things salter,
> Goats hate the halter,
> One twist of a whisker,
> A light wench 'll falter,'

and the devil shook these two in the same bottle. The further they went the more they wanted, and in the end Nadiezhda went off with Prokoudin. On the day of the Elevation of the Cross, before dinner, the policeman broke in and collected a whole cartload of goods and the case with silver.

'Why, my pet,' Agapevna said, ' our Ivan Semyonovitch got hold of the case and would not let go. They broke out into the street twice and then that fellow pushed him. Before my dear saw what was happening he was off the steps and fell against the water-butt and how the water splashed, and he got hold of the water-piping and the pipe came off and down he went on his side before he knew what was happening. " It 's all right," he says, " I don't understand—yes, a hand,—lead me, Agapevna ! " and burst into tears. And that bitch of a Nadyorka sits on the cart and guffaws, and says " What do I want with you, you rotten bald old devil, there are younger ones ! " And all round the people were making mock, there were about forty, the shame of it! And so, my pet, all through a woman he had such suffering. Now he is in hospital.'

The next day Zimarev went to the hospital. It was already late, and past the visiting hour, but as he was an official they let him in.

Stratilatov recognized his friend, but it was difficult to recognize him. He was lying on a bed with his side swathed in bandages, unable to turn or lift a hand, like a block of wood. And not rosy, but all darkened,—and not that black down, but grey whiskers bristled; and it was obvious now that hitherto he had dyed them and cut them short himself; and a prickly beard was on him and his dull little eyes, like two glass beads, winked to and fro, bent in towards his nose.

' I am not sorry about my side, Boris Sergeyevitch, but because that villainous woman took the silver. If I was not ill I should go straight to the office,' was all Ivan Semyonovitch could say, and it was obvious his side gave him great pain.

And, looking at his friend with those dull eyes, it seemed he was asking all the time :

' And why do people quarrel; what do they struggle for ; and how can you know who is right and when it will all end ? '

But the spasm passed, and he repeated :

' I am not sorry about my side, Boris Sergeyevitch.'

It broke up Ivan Semyonovitch. His time had come, and he did not even see the first snow, did not renew his raccoon coat, did not win through.

On the first day of Theodore Studites, when the Winter winds blow down from the iron mountains, he communed, took the extreme unction, and died.

People said that he was in great pain before his death, and weary in spirit. He constantly complained that he was unable to arrest his thoughts, and it sorely oppressed his eyes; and it seemed that some sort of people shaped like spades rush at him and tie him with ropes under the arms, and drag him like a cur to the river to drown him; and he resists and howls but they drag him their way without one word. And then as if a crow keeps circling above him, a black herald, an iron nose and copper legs, and opens its bill and lower and lower bends it downwards. And the Sheesheega's tail appears to him flashing in the yard, or in the corner like a chimney, smoky, downy, like old Tom's —there, there, oh, it will smother him.

'I-va-a-a-n! V-a-a-s-si-i-li! Pyo-o-o-tr!' Ivan Semyonovitch chanted, calling on either dead he wished to remember or living friends; and then would lie petrified, still as a post.

And when the last hour was come, a minute before he died, he grew quieter and stopped his nonsense— stopped wandering, and then suddenly sprang up from the bed, straightened himself, drew himself up on those thin wiry legs, ay, and that belly all atremble. Oh, thus he stood, open-pated to the sun; and his nurse quite positively said that he began to read the prayer to the Virgin. But the assistant-surgeon Zhokhov sniggered and said it was not the Virgin prayer at all, but some sort of poem you know ;—and, as if mown down, he fell, and sweat broke out on the bridge of his nose, and a drop rolled down his nose, drop following drop, and the light was removed from his eyes—all became dark, and he went away into eternal life.

Stratilatov had no descendants, and he left no testament, and his money, ten thousand (a thousand pounds), went to the Treasury. A sale of his effects was appointed, but for the time Agapevna lived with them.

And she became like a half-witted one, the old woman now sleepless. By night she would lie down on her couch, but could not stay, and she would spring from the ante-room on to the verandah porch—and it always seemed she could hear Ivan Semyonovitch crying :

'Agapevna ? '

'Here I am, batyoushka.'